Raiders of Time

By Richard Terrain

Dedication

To Joe and Chris and their 2 beautiful children.

Prologue

DATA FILE IMAGES OF ARMAGEDDON

Images of lighting and fire. Lighting strikes buildings, destroying them. Stars explode and the planet Earth being engulfed in fire. The whole scene is one of hell and terror. We see people screaming and fleeing from some unseen horror. A small skeleton of a child lays smoking on the ground discarded toy doll next to it. We see images of millions upon millions of human skulls staring up at a night sky full of lightning accusingly. We see whole cities and towns engulfed in fire. The image like a scene from the book of Revelations describing Armageddon... As these scenes are played out, we hear a voice...

What you are seeing is what could have happened at the end of the 20th century. In fact as the year 1988 drew to a close, the human race did in fact face total Armageddon. All that stood before it was a good heroic young man called John Parker. What made this one man so special will be revealed later.

The Dark Lord of the Dark Dimension had joined an evil movement called the Reckoning Movement. Two of the members of the Dark Dimension, who were Trans – dimensional beings, who were called Kaiser and Gann put together their plans for the end of the human race in 1988. However just as it seemed they were close to completing their evil plan, John Parker found out what the Dark Dimension and The Reckoning Movement were up too. He managed to defeat the evil Dark Lords just in time. Kaiser and Gann were believed killed in the battle. It was a little after this that John discovered that his nemesis and one time sweetheart Stacey Cannon had turned to the evil Reckoning Movement and Dark Dimension to gain ultimate power.

John Parker disappeared. However, the fate of mankind is now once again to face Armageddon. However, this time the battle for the fate of Earth and mankind wouldn't be fought in the 21st century, but in Earth's past.

And once more John Parker would be needed to stop the end of the world...

RAIDERS OF TIME

DATA FILE ENGLAND, SOUTHAMPTON, IN THE YEAR 1993

THE BLACK CAT BAR/RESTAURANT. NIGHT.

John Parker a man in his early 40's is sat in a posh bar/restaurant with his friend Kim, she is 30ish and attractive in a plain sort of way. Video screens hang on the walls, showing some kind of horror music video, while creepy classical music plays in the background, which gives the place a somewhat, odd effect. John keeps on looking around him in a scared manner, Kim watches him, and worried about the way her friend is acting. Beyond them are large windows, which stare out at the wet streets outside. John chain-smokes and keeps on staring out of the window, as if expecting to see someone – or – something outside.

Kim, 'you all right John?'

John, looking up suddenly. As if from a bad dream, 'What – oh – yes I'm fine.'

Kim, 'You just looked a little spaced out, that's all.'

John, 'Really I'm fine. Just that music video is giving me the creeps. Don't see what the young se in them.'

Kim, 'Listen to you, you're sounding just like an old man.'

John, 'Well I'll be 46 soon. I'm not a young man anymore.'

Kim, 'They say life begins at 40.'

John, 'That's what they say. But does that count for people who are over 40 and had three breakdowns on their life. Or someone who's a strange, confused nutter who just happens to be a so – so writer.'

4

Kim, 'I happen to think you're a great writer. Sometimes when I read your work, I feel like you've been and done some of the things you write about. Which is a bit silly as most of your written work centres on the future or way back in the past. You never know you might be a time – traveller and not know it.'

Kim takes a sip of her drink and smiles at John.

'Sorry I must sound really silly talking like that, me talking about you being a time –traveller and such like. Hope you don't think I'm making fun. It's just that, and I'm not saying this because I'm your agent, but I just wish I could turn words into great stories like you can.'

John, 'Thank you Kim. You're very kind for saying that.'

John stares out of the large window and takes out a cigarette, he is about to light it when he stops suddenly. A scared expression closes his face. He looks around as if looking for someone.

Nothing seems out of place or wrong. Just people drinking, chatting, and eating. John looks out of the large window again. This time there is someone there. A young fair hared pretty woman. She seems to be trying to say something that John can't make out.

Then without warning the young woman is gone. She seems to disappear into thin air. In an almost comical way John turns and looks at Kim, then turns and stares back out of the window. There is no one outside, just the rain, and the wet streets. Kim is now getting worried. She lays her hand gently on Johns, and looks at him with some concern. When she speaks she talks to John, softly and gently.

Kim, 'Whatever's the matter? You look like you've just seen a ghost.'

John, 'I think I just might have. If I didn't know better, I would say I was dead drunk.'

Kim, 'Well that can't be it. You haven't touched a drop the hard stuff for years, you're tee – total. Come on tell me, what did you see? I'm starting to worry.'

John, 'I thought I saw someone outside. My eyes must be playing tricks on him or something. Please don't worry, I'm not getting ill again if that's what you're worried about. And before you ask, yes I did take my pills today. Like I do everyday.'

Kim, 'I can't help but worry sometimes. The last time you got bad, it was awful. I don't want you to ever have to go through that again.'

John, 'Please stop worrying your pretty little head over me. I'm fine honest. It could have been a side effect of the pills I take, a sort of flashback if you like. Let's just forget it, come on we better eat this food before it gets cold.'

Kim, 'Okay, let's forget it.'

She smiles fondly at John. He returns the smile and then starts to eat his meal. Kim returns to her own meal. The background music has changed to some sort of creepy version of the song 'Hello Space Boy' by David Bowie. John tries to hum along to the song, but gives up after while.

He stops eating and takes out a cigarette, lights up and takes a deep drag and smiles to himself, in an almost childish way, as if to say 'look at me I'm smoking' Kim looks up from her food and notices John smiling to himself. She lets out a little giggle.

Kim, 'You really love smoking your cigarettes don't you? Even though I know it's bad for you, I have to admit you do look pretty cool when you smoke. But having said that you really should try to give up. Or try cutting down'

John, 'Don't you start! I'll have you know I can cough my guts out each morning with such force, that I make heaven and Earth move. You tell me anyone else that can do that, and then I'll quit smoking. But here's the joke, everyone says I cough like that because I smoke too much.'

Kim, 'It is because you smoke too much, my dear.'

John, 'So my Doctor keeps on telling me. But what are you to do; everyone needs some sort of vice in their life. Tell me Kim what's you're vice in life. Too much kinky sex and randy lovemaking. Go on tell me Kim, I promise not to tell. If your lucky I might write about it in a book someday, I'll change your name of course.'

Kim laughing, 'I never seem to stay with a man long enough to find out. All my ex – boyfriends have been no good in bed, lazy, stupid, or downright lousy, or all four of those things'.

John, 'Well you could always try and be gay. Not that I would want to watch or anything. I'm too much of a gentleman for that, but you never know, it might just give you a wider outlook on life, they always say you should try everything once in your life. Then again if you turn gay, it might confuse you. You might become as strange and confused and odd as I am.'

John smiles at Kim.

'But really, you will find Mr Right someday, there's always someone for someone.
Well that's what I like to think anyway. I would like to think that there's someone out there for everyone, someone who would sweep us off our feet, and share all those magic moments in life. I'm not talking about sex, but true love, undying love. Some people like me, spend their whole life, looking, hoping, before coming to the fact it might all be just a silly dream.'

Kim smiles at John with a bright smile.

Kim, 'It sounds like a lovely dream.'

She holds up her glass.

'Here's to me finding Mr Right and you finding the woman of your dreams.'

John holds up his glass.

John, 'I'll drink to that, cheers!'

Kim, 'Cheers!'

John and Kim return to their food. The lights in the bar/restaurant dim and the music get even louder. Feeling full up, John pushes his plate away and takes out another cigarette, even through the last one he had is smouldering away in an ashtray. He lights up. A look of anxiety comes across his face. He stares up at the ceiling, a big ceiling fan, is revolving slowly above. He watches as if he is in some sort of trance or daydream.

Then almost as if with effort he looks away. Kim hasn't noticed John acting oddly.

John, 'I must say this is an unusual place. Almost gothic in some ways, I suppose the young love it though. But I can't really see anything in it. Give me a cosy Jazz joint anytime. A place with colourful sights and sounds. You know like those art – deco places they used to have in the 1930, or 40's or even the 50's for that matter. Now that I could live with.'

Kim, 'You were born after your time weren't you. I can just picture you now, as some sort of private eye – or gumshoe as you like to call them. Sitting in some speakeasy, chatting up some dame and smoking away, trying to get to the bottom of some complex case. You've always had that dream about becoming a private eye – sorry my mistake – a gumshoe.'

John, 'How did you know that I wanted to be a gumshoe?'

Kim, 'You told me once just before you had you're last breakdown. You were acting rather odd that night, as I recall.'

John, 'Can't say that I remember. Just as well really, there are some parts of my past I'd rather forget, like the subject of my breakdowns.'

Kim, 'Sorry I didn't mean to bring up old troubles.'

John smiles, 'It's all right. You didn't say anything out of place. Forget what I said. Anyway getting back to this place, don't you find it a touch morbid? You know dark, gloomy and dare I say it, grim. Now I know blacks the in colour at the moment, but it all seems a little weird, showing horror music videos and as for the music, all that creepy classical and the even more creepy versions of well known songs. The whole place seems designed to scare the hell out of people. To tell you the truth I don't feel quite right being here.'

Kim, 'How do you mean?'

John, 'Well I've felt uncomfortable here, ever since we arrived in this place tonight. Don't get me wrong; it was lovely of you to take me out to dinner. It's just that I can't seem to shift this feeling – of – I don't know, paranoia you could say. It's like I'm missing something important. I don't know how to explain it. I suppose it's like I have a plot for a book all worked out in my head, but can't seem to put the words or thoughts down on paper.'

Kim, 'Well I know to take you to a Jazz bar next time. Just try to enjoy yourself okay. You know to be frank, I sometimes feel like an old woman here myself. Sometimes I think I'm old enough to be the mother of some these people. I'm sorry I brought you here now.'

John, 'Oh it's not that bad really. It's just I think my minds playing tricks on me lately. Things have seemed a little dream – like for me for while. I keep on having these dreams about the end of the world. Strange thing is in the dreams I'm younger. Not that that really explains anything. So I decided I'll go and see my Doctor the other say. I was going to tell you sooner, but I knew you would get all worked up and worried –'

Kim, cutting in, 'What did he say?'

John, 'Oh the usual, the stress of writing a new book and little things in life getting the top of me. He said things like that sometimes cause the mind to play tricks on you.'

Kim, 'What did he say you should do about it?'

John, 'What do you think? He sent me away with even more pills. I feel more like a pill junkie now, than I normally do.'

Kim, 'But you have been taking them. Your pills I mean.'

John, 'Of course I have.'

Kim, 'Are you sure?'

John sharply, 'Have I never lied to you, for God's sake! I know better than not to take them!

Kim, 'Sorry. I do believe you. It's just you've been out of sorts tonight. No one likes to see his or her friends getting ill, you know.'

John, 'Sorry I didn't mean to snap.'

He gives a gesture of apology.

'I apologise, you know what us writers are like. Always making a mould – hill. Am I forgiven?'

Kim smiles at him kindly.

'All right, I forgive you. Only on count of you being so old and long in the tooth.'

John, 'You say the kindest things my dear.'

Kim watches as John takes out yet another cigarette from a new pack, and lights it up. John notices Kim staring at him. He looks at her apologetically.

Kim, 'Don't mind me, it's your life and lungs remember. I hope you don't mind me saying his, but you're home stinks of cigarette smoke.'

John, almost childishly 'It does. It really does. You must come over again and take a whiff, give you're clothes a 'lived' in smell.'

Kim laughs gently and takes a sip of her drink. John takes a few drags on his smoke. He looks around the bar, as if looking for something.

John, suddenly, intently, '*The Reckoning Movement and The Dark Lords of the Dark Dimension must be stopped!*

John has spoken so suddenly and unexpectedly, that Kim looks up at him startled.

Kim, after a moment, 'Sorry I didn't quite catch that.'

John, whispering, almost in some sort of trance, *'They are planning another apocalypse! To allow a New Order to rise from the ashes of the dead!'*

Kim a little taken aback, 'What are you talking about John?'

John seems to snap out of his trance – like state. He looks at Kim for a moment as if he doesn't know who she is. He shakes his head, as if trying to clear it.

John, 'I don't know what I'm talking about myself. Why on earth would I say something like that? This is all very strange.'

Kim looks around the bar, as if looking for someone who might be able to help, while she is doing this, John without warning, winces in pain and holds his head in his hands. He winces in pain again. This time Kim notices his discomfort.

Kim, 'Hey! You okay there John?'

John speaking as if in a great deal of pain, *'God what's happening to me? Please Kim I think I need a Doctor.'*

John closes his eyes, as if somehow to block out the pain. When he opens them, he looks around in shock.

His surroundings have changed. Kim is no longer at his table – in fact he is no longer in the Black Cat bar. He is now in some sort Jazz bar joint, right out of a 1930's, 40's, movie. The place is full of people dressed in the clothes of the 30's and 40's eras, who all seem be drinking, chatting. They don't take any notice of John. John looks around him in shock, not quite able to take in what's happening.

A young fair –haired, pretty waitress walks up to John's table. John stares at her in disbelief, for this is the same young woman that he had seen earlier outside the window of the Black Cat bar. The waitress smiles brightly at him.

'Hi there. Can I get you anything Sir? Beer or something a little stronger perhaps?' the waitress asked in a gentle US accent.

John stares at her.

John, 'What?'

Waitress, 'Can I get you a drink sir?'

John, 'Ah…no. I was just leaving. Look this might sound a little odd, strange even. But what's the name of this place? And what year it is?'

The waitress stares at him for a moment, and then grins.

'As if you didn't already know. I've heard some chat – up lines before, but that's a new one.'

John, 'Could you please humour me?'   '

Waitress, 'Well if you insist, well this is 'Rick's Place' the best bar in the whole of the U.S.A and the year is 1949.'

John, 'U.S.A.! You mean to tell me I'm in the states, and it's the year 1949.'

The waitress laughs gently.

'Yep you're in the good old U.S. of A. I kind of like this game. Just because you're cute. You sure you don't want a drink? It'll be on the house, my treat.'

John, 'No. That's really all right. I've been tee – total for years. Drink and the hard stuff never really agreed with me. Listen could you tell me where I could find a place to stay, for the night. A hotel or something.'

John thinks for a moment.

John, 'Not that my money will be any good here though.'

Waitress her eyes lighting up, 'You're British aren't you? God I love the way you British talk.'

The waitress stares at him for a moment.

'Why do you think you're money won't be any good around here?'

John thinks fast.

'Ah…What I meant was that I seem to have mislaid my wallet. It was in my pocket a moment ago. Lord knows what's happened to it.'

11

The waitress looked shocked, 'Really! I hate to say this, but I think you might have been had. You get pick – pockets everywhere these days.'

She looks at John with concern.

'What are you going to do now?'

John, 'Lord knows. This is all like a dream, well more like a nightmare really. I keep on hoping I might wake up soon.'

The waitress seems to think something over. She goes and sits across from John at his table.

Waitress, 'Listen I don't normally do this. But I've always prised myself on being able to tell good people from the bad ones. And seem like a very sweet guy. I'll tell you what; you can stay at my place tonight. That's if you want too that is. And tomorrow you can get yourself sorted out. But don't expect anything else. I'm not that type of girl, I'll warn you now; I'm a girl who knows how to handle herself. But I have a feeling you're not the type to try anything. You seem too much of a gentleman for that. So what do you say?'

John thinks over the offer, and then he smiles and nods.

John, 'Well all right and don't worry. I'll be out of your life tomorrow. You're very kind'.

The waitress laughed, 'Believe me I can be a bitch at times. Well my name's Kate Anderson, what's yours?'

John smiled

'My name's John Parker, and I'm delighted to meet you Miss Anderson.'

Kate, 'And I'm delighted to meet such a nice guy. Look I'm finishing in a few minutes; do you want any pop or anything?'

John looks at her confused.

'Pop?'

Kate smiles and looks at him as if he's from another planet.

Kate, 'Yeah pop, you know cola – cola or something. You said you were tee –total.'

John, 'Oh I see. Yes coke will be fine, thank you.'

Kate checked her watch, 'Okay, I'll get someone to bring your drink over to you. I'll see you in a bit all right.'

John, 'Okay.'

Kate gets up from her seat and walks off. He watches her for a moment and then takes out a cigarette and lights up. He is surprised to find his hands are shaking.

He looks around a bar and notices two shifty looking men, in black suits sat at a table, a little way from him. They seem to be whispering to each other, and every so often they turn and stare at John. John looks away uneasy.

A male voice makes him jump.

'Here's your drink sir, on the house.'

John looks up to see a young waiter smiling at him. John forces a smile.

John, 'Thank you very much.'

'You're welcome.' *The young man walks off clearly bored with his job. John looks back at the table where the two men in suits had been sitting. They have gone. John looks around but can't see any sign of them. He notices Kate coming back to his table she has a coat on. He smiles warmly at her, glad to see a familiar face.*

John, 'Hello again.'

Kate smiled, 'Miss me?'

John forced a smile, 'More than you know.'

Kate looked out at the rain filled street outside the window, 'Well are you ready to go? If we're lucky we should be able to get a cab outside.'

John, 'Lead on Kate.'

With that they leave the bar.

KATE'S APARTMENT. NIGHT.

Kate's apartment is a largish, cosy place. John stands in the middle of the floor, looking a little awkward and uncomfortable, not quite knowing what to do. Kate notices his discomfort and smiles, she points to a sofa.

'Please have a seat. Make yourself at home.'

John nods and takes a seat on the sofa.

Kate, 'You can smoke if you like if you like. I'll just go and get you an ashtray. Can I get you a drink, while I'm at it?'

John, 'Water will be fine, thanks'.

Kate goes into another room, and returns with an ashtray and a glass of drink a few moments later. John takes the drink and takes a sip. He looks around the apartment and notices at black and white picture of a pretty young woman, hanging on the wall.

John points at the picture.

'Do you mind if I ask who that picture is of?'

Kate, 'Oh that. That's my mother. She died when I was very young. She's kind of cute isn't she? Don't you think?'

John, 'Very. You take after her.'

Kate, 'What about you? Do you have any family?'

John thinks for a moment, a hunted expression crosses his face.

'I know this is going to sound strange, but I can't remember. Isn't that odd, but this whole evening has been far from normal.'

John looks and notices Kate staring intently at him. Something about the stare gives John the creeps. John tries smiling at her, but she continues to stare at him. Then after a moment she leans over and whispers to him.

Kate, 'Do you know how you got here, John?'

John, 'We got here by cab didn't we?'

Kate, 'No, I mean do you know how you got to this time, this era, 1949.'

John, 'I really don't know what you're talking about.'

Kate, 'You were in the year 2015, two hours ago, now you're here in 1949. One of the time periods you most like writing about. Can you explain why you're here?'

John looks at her in shock and amazement.

John, 'How do you know that I was in the year 2015? I never told you anything. Who are you?'

Kate, 'I'm someone who can help you. Don't worry I didn't bring you here to hurt you, or anything. To be honest you might not believe what I have to tell you. But I'll try to explain as best as I can. There is a secret world – wide Federation called Enigma. Which I will tell you more about later. Enigma were doing experiments dealing with time – travel –'

John cutting in, 'Time travel. What is this, some kind of joke? Listen –'

Kate cutting in sharply, 'No! You listen. We might not have a lot of time. So please just shut up and listen. Everything about you're past is a lie. Why is that you can't remember anything about your childhood. Haven't you ever wondered about that?

John looks at not able to take in what she's talking about. Kate goes speaking more gently this time.

'Please I know this must be hard for you, but just try and follow what I'm saying. You work for Enigma, you are one of its best agents, you have many gifts, one of which is that you are a master time – traveller. Enigma's beginnings are over three millennia old. It has always been in charge of Earth's affairs, protecting this planet from horror that you can only dream of. You are one of the people who protect the human race from these terrors.

 You were one of the first successful time – travellers. When it was decided that the best way to defeat some of our enemies was through time – travel, we had to breed an army of time – travellers. However some of the early time – experiments came up with unexpectected problems. But while that was going on, Enigma had bigger problems, things got out of control. Certain factors broke away from Enigma and created they're own movement. As with any rouge power movement they have a name. They call themselves The Reckoning Movement.

This evil movement is on the brink of destroying all the good Enigma has done for man – kind. I've lost count of how many times you stopped them, from carrying out their evil plans. But you disappeared after you're last encounter with the Reckoning Movement and the Dark Dimension –'

John cutting in, 'What's the Dark Dimension?

Kate, 'I'll get to that in a moment. It took us a while but we managed to track you down in the year 2015. We had to time – teleport you here to 1949. We only ever do that as a last resort, but we couldn't send a time – ship to 2015, in case we were tracked. But we need you're help, we think the Reckoning Movement are planning another insane plan. We believe you have information about it. We weren't expecting your mind to be so confused however. But you're our only hope.'

John, 'If I'm to believe what I'm hearing, then surly if Enigma has such power and technology, then you can stop this – what did you call them – Reckoning Movement yourself!'

Kate, 'Technology and power is of no use, if you don't have the wisdom to use it for good.'

John, 'What's that supposed mean?'

Kate, 'It's something you once said. Believe me John, there's information that your mind holds, that could save the human race.'

John, 'I don't know what you're talking about. I don't have any such information. This really is getting beyond a joke now. I'm just a writer, a writer for god sake!'

Kate, 'If you really believe that, then it may already be to late. Because believe me you're far, far from being just a writer. The information inside your mind could hold the key to everything.'

John, 'And I'm to believe that the all-powerful Enigma doesn't have any clue to what this information is.'

Kate, 'We we're hoping you could tell us. We believe you found out something about a Reckoning Movement plan on one of you're time travels. We really need to know what the Reckoning Movement is planning. Please think, John, think! Do you remember anything? Anything at all.'

John, 'All I remember is waking up this morning with one hell of a headache, doing some housework, then some writing. And this evening meeting a friend of mine for dinner at a dive of a place. It was there things started to get odd, I started to hear and see things. Before I ended up here in 1949.'

Kate shaking her head, 'None of that helps. The first part is the life you must have set up for yourself in the future. The second part about seeing and saying odd things is the side effects of the illness you were given when you were born, so you could time – travel. The last part is us teleporting you here to 1949 –'

John cutting in, 'Wait a minute. You said I was given an 'illness' when I was born. What illness?'

Kate doesn't seem to hear what John has just asked.

Kate talking to herself, 'This is worse than I thought. Could be some sort of amnesia brought on by some sort of stress –'

John, cutting in, sharply, shouting, 'What illness was I given as a child!'

Kate is silent for a moment, looking uncomfortable. Then she answers John. Speaks in almost a whisper…

'You were given artificially induced Schizophrenia, a few hours after you were born.'

John, 'What are you talking about? 'Just after you were born, the Enigma Federation gave you artificiality induced Schizophrenia.'

John, 'Why the hell would anyone want to do such a thing? And to a new born of all things.'

Kate, 'John we really don't have time for this.'

John, shouting, sharply, 'Tell me!'

Kate, 'All right. All right, I'll tell you. Enigma needed human subjects with Schizophrenia. They needed to modify the illness, to allow the human subjects to travel through the time – vortex. I don't know the whole story or all the facts. But it had something to do with the fact, that the human subjects who were able to do this were harboured with this modified Schizophrenia developed certain chemical imbalances with in the brain and body.

The Enigma Master's found those with this upgraded form of the illness, could with stand the side effects of time – travel the pain, trauma, the whole effect of it. But the truth is no one really know why this is, why the subjects that were given this upgraded Schizophrenia were so perfect for time – travel. Just that they were.

The human subject members who didn't have the illness, died with in hours, sometimes minutes of entering the time – vortex. So it was decided that for the good of mankind, that Enigma would breed newborns and the healthiest would be given this modified upgraded, form of Schizophrenia, so that they could be trained to become master time – travellers.

But in your case something strange happened, along with ability to time – travel, you developed other powers, the power to sense things that others couldn't, the power to move objects with you're mind alone. You also showed the ability to cloud people's minds and such like. You are one of the greatest agents Enigma has ever had. Believe me, in some ways when you were given that illness, it was a blessing not a curse.'

'Anyway you were one of the subjects that always happy and willing to work for Enigma. However this wasn't the case for all the subjects. When some of the subjects found out why they had been brought into this world, they were far from happy and they rebelled and formed the Reckoning Movement.

Legend has it that a very nasty race of aliens from a place that we call The Dark Dimension offered their services to the Reckoning Movement in exchange for – well we don't really know, all I can tell you that these aliens from the Dark Dimension are bad news, they are akin to the Nazi's of this world.'

John, 'Well that's a nice story and puts your great Enigma Federation in a nice light doesn't it. How do I know you're telling me the truth, about me being happy to work for Enigma, you would say that wouldn't you. I get the feeling this Enigma Federation doesn't give a damn about anyone. They seem to like using humans like some kind of experimental fodder. As if human beings were some form of guinea pigs.'

Kate, 'No! You've got it all wrong. It's not what you think. Enigma did for the good of mankind. Listen we really don't have time for this right now. When this is all over and we get you're memory back, then I'll be more than happy to talk to you about the pros and cons of what Enigma does.

But for now we have to get along and work together to stop whatever the Reckoning Movement is planning. So I need to know right now, can I count on you just trusting me and you helping me out. Believe me the Reckoning Movement are scrum of the universe. They must never be allowed to succeed in their goal for world power and the control of time.

Please John, I need your help here. So what do you say?'

John stares at Kate for a moment thinking things over. He takes out a cigarette and lights it. He takes drag and then lets out a sigh and smiles.

John, 'All right. I'll help you. If you'll telling me the truth about me having these powers, and I can sense things, then I'm sensing you'll telling me the truth. I just hope I'm not making a big mistake, by thinking that Enigma is the good side, when The Reckoning Movement are the good guys all along. But if I have to trust someone in all this mess, then I suppose I could do a lot worse than trust a pretty young woman.

So what do we do now? Do we use hidden codes and meet in dark alleyways and speak into phones at midnight. Like they do in all those spy books and films.'

Kate, 'Not quite. First we have to find out what you know. And I suppose the best way to do that is through using a mind probe.'

John, 'Ah…yes the mind probe. I was just going to say that. Can I just ask something Kate?'

Kate, 'Sure go ahead.'

John, 'Just what is a mind probe?'

Kate, 'It's a device used to find out hidden information with in the brain, facts that may somehow have been blocked or wiped from the subject's memory.'

John, 'Okay there are two other things I want to ask. First do we have to go to Enigma to do this? –'

Before John can finish what he is saying, Kate waves her hands over her mother's picture on the wall. The wall slides back to reveal a secret hidden room, which holds futuristic consoles and hi – tech technology with in it. A chair with some sort of device hanging above it stands in the middle of the room. John stares at the room and the chair. Kate smiles at him and gives him a cute wink.

Kate, 'No we don't have to go to Enigma to do the mind probe. We have everything we need right here. Don't worry it's not as scary as it looks.'

John nods slowly. He takes a puff on his cigarette and walk over to the centre of the hidden room. He reaches out and touches the chair, as if to make sure it's real.

Kate, 'You said you had two things to ask me. What was the second thing you wanted to know?'

John, 'Will this hurt?'

Kate smiles at John Kate, 'Ah…I was kind of hoping you wouldn't ask me that.'

SIDEWALK OUTSIDE KATE'S APARTMENT. NIGHT

A black car sits parked on the road outside Kate's apartment. The car's windows are blacked out.

RECKONING MOVEMENT AGENTS CAR. NIGHT

The two men dressed in black suits that John saw before at the bar are sat staring at the lit windows at Kate's home. After a moment Reckoning Movement Agent One speaks.

RECKONING MOVEMENT (R.M.) AGENT ONE, 'Well I think it's time we paid Miss Anderson a call don't you think agent Shadow?'

Agent Shadow nods and takes out a gun- like device from a pocket on his coat.

R.M. AGENT TWO, 'I'm sure she'll be happy enough to see us at this time at night…'

R.M. AGENT ONE, 'Remember it's the man we want. Miss Anderson is just a bonus…'

KATE'S APARTMENT. NIGHT

John is sat in the chair the device over the chair is now covering the upper half of his head. Energy starts to generate from the device and John begins to glow.

While this is going on Kate is stood staring at a screen on a console.

Kate, 'The pain should subside in a moment or two John. Just try to relax and ride out the pain.'

John twitches in pain a few moments more and is then still. Kate checks the read out on the screen.

Kate, 'You should embark on a short of vivid flashback in a few seconds; try to tell me everything you see. Okay?'

As Kate says this, we embark on John's flashback.

FLASHBACK

GESTAPO HEADQUARTERS. 1939. NIGHT

We are outside the Berlin headquarters of the Gestapo; it is a handsome mansion in Prinz Albrechtstrasse. We see things from John's P.O.V. The pleasant tree-lined street is completely empty. No one passes the Gestapo headquarters. A cordon of fear surrounds the building.

From John's point of view. We see him pass armed SS guards on the door and go into the building

GESTAPO HEADQUARTERS. NIGHT

We see John go up some stairs. He goes to an outer office with yet another guard on the door; he goes over to a severe- looking bespectacled female behind a desk. The female points to a row of hard chairs against a wall and she returns to her work.

John goes over to one of the chairs and sits down and waits. The female after a moment picks up an office telephone. After a low- voiced conversation she puts down the phone and talks frostily.

'A member of the Fuehrer shall see you now Herr Parker.'

John walks past the armed guar and enters an office. It is a simple room, furnished in plain dark colours. Heavy curtains are drawn against the night; a single light leaves the room gloomy and shadowed giving the air a creepy fee. At a desk at the end of the room sits Loker a neat black uniformed figure. He looks up as John enters. He gives John an icy smile.

Loker, 'I welcome you in the name of Fuehrer and the Reckoning Movement. We have much to talk about.

To start off with we shall talk about how much you know about the Movement and our plans and of course there is also the matter of the information you have of our Brothers of the apocalypse.'

John just stares ahead, it is clear from the expression on his face he is trying to hold back giving out the facts he knows. Loker smiles...

'Really John, didn't you wonder way you came here to Berlin. We control your very thoughts and actions through our psychics. Powerful psychics that we have brought up since birth, but even we have to admit that your mind is much more powerful than we first thought...which makes us wonder just how powerful your gifts are...they could be of great use to the Fuehrer. You become of a member of are super race...if you like it or not...we have such plans for you my friend...such plans...'

SUDDENLY WE RETURN TO...

KATE'S APARTMENT. NIGHT.

John screams out, the device lifts from his head. Kate rushes over and helps him hold of the chair...she helps steadily him a look of...almost love in her expression John stares at her...his face close to her...for a moment they look as if they might kiss...but John pulls away. Kate goes over and gets a glass of water.

She hands him the glass...

Kate, 'Here drink this...it'll make you feel better.'

John takes a few sips.

John, 'Well did you find anything of use...using that machine of yours?'

Kate shakes her head.

'No nothing I didn't already know...'

John cutting in gently, 'I'm sorry I couldn't be of more use.'

Kate smiles at him fondly.

Kate, 'Don't be so hard on yourself. From what I gather they used very powerful psychics to enter your mind and thoughts. I've had it done a few times to me as well...I know the feeling you feel used...there's a team for it we call it mind rage...because that's what it is...being forced to do something a against your will. Still we know they were after something that you knew...something had them worried that's for sure. If we are to find out what that 'something' is we'll going to have to unblock your memory pathways. Something or the other has put a powerful mind block...or force field around your mind... '

John looks her almost like an ashamed child.

'I'm sorry Kate...I really don't remember anything apart from what you saw. Is there anyway to unblock this force field of whatever it is.'

Kate thinks for a moment...and suddenly breaks into a grin.

Kate, 'The Invidious...of course that's the answer...why didn't I think of it before.'

John looks at confused.

John, 'What's the Invidious?'

Kate smiles brightly and kisses John on the cheek that takes him by surprise.

Kate, grins, 'The Invidious my dear John...is the answer to all our worries.'

Kate stops talking as an alarm sounds throughout the room. Kate rushes over to a console.

Kate, '*R.M. Agent's* just as I thought...we'd better make tracks. '

John, '*R.M. Agent's*. Now why doesn't that sound good?'

Kate, 'It's short for Reckoning Movement Agents. I'll explain more about them later. I'd better active the teleport gate.'

Without warning Kate's front door is kicked in. The two R.M. Agent's that were in the in the car earlier on... stand framed in the doorway. They open fire...laser bolts rock the apartment.

Kate quickly presses a button on a console...just as John throws himself to the floor as a laser bolt misses him by an inch. The wall to the hidden room closes cutting off the laser fire.

John gets up to feet and watches as Kate pulls down a lever on a wall.

A pyramid of light appears in front of them. It is about eight feet tall and glows with unearthly white light. John stares at it in wonder.

Behind the closed wall the sounds of the lasers gets louder.

Kate, 'I really think we should get out of here...that wall won't keep them out for long...'

John stares at the pyramid of light not seeming to care what Kate has said.

John,' with childlike wonder, 'What is that thing?'

Kate, 'It's a teleport gate. Always compactly handy when you want to make a quick exit…now stop staring at and follow me and hurry.'

Kate rushes into the pyramid of light and John follows …and it disappears into nothing.

Just as the R.M. Agent's break into the room.

They look around and discover that they're pray has been lost.

They scream inhumanly.

DATA FILE THE INVIDIOUS

INVIDIOUS. DARK SIDE OF EARTH'S MOON OBRIT.

We are in the control room of the star ship/ time ship called the Invidious. The control room of the ship combines gothic design with the futuristic. Kate goes over to what appears to be the main control console.

John looks around in wonder at awe at the size of the place and sight of the Earth visible on a large display screen. He notices that on one side of the display there are dates and numbers, which mean nothing to him.

John, in awe 'What is this place Kate…It's strange it's almost as if it feels like I've been here before…it feels like 'home''

Kate looks up from the console she's working on and smiles at John's expression of wonder.

Kate, 'this, my Dear John is the Invidious. The flagship of the Federation a time ship, which you designed in your teens… Only one of its kind was ever built. You really are a genius John.'

John, 'you sure you have the right person? I've never thought of myself as a genius.'

Suddenly out of nowhere a rather cheeky metallic voice cuts in…

'It's good to see you safe and sound Master Parker, all systems are working and time drive and hyper drive are on level yellow...As always I'm more clever than the human mind'

John spins around trying to find the source of the voice. Kate notices John looking around and smiles at him. She points to a machine shaped like a pyramid at the end of the control room.

Kate, 'That's Rogue. The Invidious master computer... You could say it's a little imperfect. Rogue can be a little mischievous at times.'

Rogue, 'You say the kindest things Miss Anderson. Why don't you dump your boyfriend and fly away with me? I'm programmed to be smarter than Master Parker...'

Kate, 'Behave Rogue you will upset John... You know he's always looking for a reason to replace you...'

John, 'Why would I want to replace it, him?'

Kate, 'Oh you programmed him to care for me, so you wouldn't worry about someone taking care of me, when you were on a solo mission etc. I need to tell you something, we're ah more than friends...Long story but here's the quick version.

It took you a while to show your feelings towards me. You were hurt by your ex- Stacey Cannon. She really hurt you, she betrayed you for her own means, even switched sides to the Reckoning Movement.

She almost caused the end of the world. You loved her so much; it broke my heart to see what she did to you...

Anyway it took a while and we fell in love. Best thing that ever happened to me.'

John,' all this is so surreal, time machines, all powerful movements. I'm sorry Kate I just don't remember anything.'

Kate smiles and walks over to an open hatch. Beyond the hatch is some sort of chamber.

Kate, 'If I'm right this chamber will restore your memory. It really works in the same way as the mind probe, but it's a lot more powerful. It should if it works all right, sort of give you a jump-start. Are you okay with that?'

John, 'Will it hurt as much as the minds probe?'

Rogue, 'I will adjust the power levels to a safe level, it might sting a little, well quite a lot really…'

John gives Rogue a stare and then smiles at Kate. He walks over and enters the chamber.

John, 'I'm fine by all means do whatever you have to do…'

Kate touches a control on a control console. She lowers a lever and lightning fills the chamber causing sparks to fly about. John Parker starts to glow and falls to the ground and starts to convulse and shake. Kate stares on and has to turn away, unable to watch any further…

John screams out in terribly agony and the sounds of the screams echoes around the ship then it is over. Everything is still; the hatch way opens and from out of the chamber walks John Parker.

He walks over to Kate and takes hold of her and kisses her passionately, he now has the manner of someone not to be reckoned with. There is a powerful era about him.

He looks trim and fit, confident and alert – He absolutely radiates power and charisma.

John, 'I remember everything. You, the Federation, the Reckoning Group and the Dark Dimension… I had just found out the Reckoning Movement and the Dark Dimension had joined forces.

They're planning something big in 1939. We must stop them at any cost.'

Kate, 'Do you know who's behind this plan? Or what the plan is?'

John, 'I did think it was Stacey Cannon up to her old tricks. But then I sensed it was an old enemy of mine called Kaiser, he tempted Stacey to join the Dark Dimension in 1999. I can't be sure I thought Kaiser was destroyed in '99, but everything seems to point to his handy work. But I also get the feeling Stacey's working behind the shadows…'

Kate, 'So what do we do?'

John, 'we'll take the Invidious back to 1939, Germany. Whatever or whoever is planning to put this plan in motion it will be at the start of the war. I want you to find out anything you can about a place called 'Aryan Research Bureau'. Sense that's where some of our answers will lay. Just be careful okay?'

Kate laughs gently at John's concerns.

Kate, 'Me? Careful is my middle name remember?'

KRONPRINZENSTRASSE. STREET. DAY

A teleport gate appears and Kate dressed in the cloths of the era walks along a wide tree lined boulevard. She finds the address she is seeking a big old house set back from the road. Cautiously Kate goes up the path to the front door. To one side of the door is a small brass plate, which reads:

DOCTOR KAISER: ARYON RESEARCH BUREAU

Beneath the brass plate there is something that looks like an extra large bell- push. Kate pushes it without results for a while before she realizes you are supposed to pull it.
She gives a good heave and it comes free of its socket revealing a few inches of the rusty wire. A bell clangs somewhere in the house and with surprising speed the door opens.
An extremely unpleasant looking man peers out at her. He is a middle aged and middle size he has a high forehead and perpetually sneering expression.

Man, 'Don't you know its Sunday? We're closed!'

Kate, brightly, 'I've got an invitation'.

Kate produces an engraved card and holds it out. The man takes the card and produces a pair of round glasses with incredibly thick lenses. Putting them on he peers suspiciously at Kate.

Man, 'You're not John Parker.'

Kate, 'I'm his partner. His girlfriend so to speak... He had to go to a meeting.'

Man, 'Well Doctor Kaiser's been called away as well.'

Kate smiles sweetly at the man.

Kate, 'Right then. It's just the two of us then, any chance of a look around?'

The man takes off his glasses and stands still for a moment. It is almost as if he is listening for messages from some other place. Then he speaks...

Man, creepily, 'All right, come in then if you really want to.

He opens the door and stands aside beckoning her to enter.

INVIDIOUS CONTROL ROOM.

John is pacing up and down. He has a worried expression on his face. He looks at Rogue...

John, 'Well don't just sit there. Say something.'

Rogue, 'Such as Master Parker?'

John, 'I don't know. Ask me something, anything. Anything to pass the time...'

Rogue, 'So as to take your mind off the danger you've put Miss Anderson in, Master Parker?'

John stares at Rogue. The Master computer lets out a few sad beeps and speaks...

Rogue, 'Sorry, didn't mean to say that… I'm just as worried as you are Mister Parker.
All right. Tell me about Stacey Cannon, the woman that almost destroyed you and mankind? I've never got the chance to meet her. You were very close to her at one time weren't you?'

John lets out a sad sigh.

John, 'You really are an odd machine aren't you? Well where do I start about Stacey Cannon? I loved her once before she turned over to the dark side. I should have read the signs more early. She always was a tearaway. Even when we were younger…'

Rogue, 'Tell me about your past with her. I would love to know.'

John embarks on a flashback.

FLASHBACK:

John, 'Many years ago when I was a student studying space/ time dynamics…'

ENIGMA FEDERATION ACADEMY. DAY.

A young John, eager, curious, naïve and a young Stacey Cannon already knowing and conceited are listening to their teacher they are both clearly bored with the lesson.

Teacher, 'You have a good deal to learn yet. We all do. Learning is the greatest adventure you can go on. I'll see you in class tomorrow. Class dismissed.'

After the teacher leaves Stacey and John make a rush pact to steal a primitive time ship and make an unauthorized trip in Earth's history.

Young Stacey, 'I'm going to steal a time ship and travel through Earth's history. Come with me.'

Young John, with fear, 'But…'

Young Stacey, 'Are you afraid?'

Young John, defensively, 'Well no, but…'

Young John, 'Good. Then it's a pact.'

TIME SHIP PORT. DAY

Stacey and an uneasy looking John are in a huge port that holds the prototype primitive time ships that were built before the Invidious.

Young John, 'This is stupid; we'll never get into one of those ships. We need a teleport key. '

Young Stacey, taking out a teleport key from her pocket, 'I know that's why I stole this one.'

Stacey opens a primitive teleport gate to one of the time ships. Stacey steps into the gate first and disappears. Before John joins her, the Teacher that had been teaching them in class steps from the shadows and draws his attention to the moral aspects of space-time travel.

Teacher, 'You will find yourself in a position of great responsibility Mister Parker. You may be required to exercise moral judgement. Do not undertake this lightly! I sense great things for you Mister Parker; you always were a good kind and carrying student.'

John smiles at the Teacher and is about to step into the teleport gate when the Teacher speaks again…

Teacher, 'Just one more thing before you go Mister Parker… do you have feelings for Miss Cannon?'

John looks confused for a moment and answers carefully…

YOUNG JOHN, 'I suppose I do. We are very good friends.'

Teacher, intensely, 'Keep your friends close but keep your enemies closer. Sometimes the two blur. Just be careful my young student'

Young John, 'I'll… be careful Father.'

The Teacher studies young John's face for a moment. Then steps back into the shadows. John thinks about what the Teacher has just said for a moment an uneasy expression upon his face.

With that John steps into the teleport gate and disappears.

John, 'It was while we made a trip far back into Earth's past. That I saw a shadow on what Stacey would become. And the Teacher's words started to take on some meaning.'

EGYPT. 3000 B.C. NIGHT.

John and Stacey watch as a slave is falsely accused of stealing some food. A crowd has gathered the slave to be punished; John and Stacey both know that the slave is innocent.

Young John, 'Shouldn't we do something? I mean we both saw who really stole the food.'

Young Stacey, 'Yes, I mean no! Let's watch and see what will happen.'

The slave is beaten and beheaded. John unable to stand what he has just seen throws up. Stacey sighs and gives him a look unmoved by his emotion.

Young Stacey sarcastically, 'Have you quite finished? It's not as if he knew him or anything.'

John, 'But that man was innocent, we both saw somebody else steal the food they killed an innocent man…'

Stacey calmly, creepily, 'A minor detail…'

JOHN

After that incident in Egypt Stacey and me grew apart, but she wouldn't give up so easily even after I tried to end our relationship. She became obsessive and uncontrollable so much so she was exiled from the Enigma Federation. It was a little while before my adventure in 1999 that I last saw her again.

Even then I thought I could help her, even though Katie told me she was a lost cause. There was another night a long time ago, one fateful night abroad a beautiful and vast leisure ship called the Titanic that I was come across my old nemesis again.'

TITANIC. NIGHT.

The Titanic is sailing through the night.

TITANIC RESTAURANT. NIGHT.

John is having a great time with some friends, when suddenly he spots Stacey staring from across the room. There is something visibly more sinister about her now. Stacey walks over to John's table and whispers into his ear…

Stacey, 'Would you care for a dance my Dear John?'

John, 'You've got some cheek. I should haul you to the Federation. You have broken every law in the universe not to mention all the people you have killed. You're insane.'

Stacey doesn't seem to have heard any of John's words and she leans closer and she whispers creepily...

Stacey, 'I really think you should give me a dance, for old time sake besides people's lives could depend on it.'

Sensing that he has no choice. John follows her to the dance floor and they start to dance. Stacey watches him intensely like a cat with a mouse. The stare makes John uncomfortable.

John, 'What's this all about, Stacey? What do you want?'

Stacey, 'Have you ever thought about changing history John? I mean what does the History books tell you about this wonderful ship?'

John, 'Nothing that great... It's just a leisure ship that made a trip from Southampton, England to New York.'

Stacey, 'What if I said I have changed the course of history so that the ship hits an iceberg and sinks killing thousands of people?'

John looks at her uneasily.

John, 'I'd say you were wrong, it would take someone more powerful than you with your little party tricks to change history that much. I read up on this voyage before I teleported down here, nothing what you said ever happened doubt you could cause a disaster of that force.'

Stacey, 'Well, I think you're in for a surprise something should happen right about now!'

Before John can say anything else the disaster occurs as predicted. In the mayhem that follows, John tries to help as many people as he can to get to the lifeboats, he then confronts Stacey angrily.

John, 'You're insane! You caused all this! Why? Why?'

Stacey, smiles evilly, 'to show you how much more powerful than you I have become. I have powers like that of a God now and you and your pathetic Enigma Federation will soon be no more. I give you this glorious disaster as a gift and as a warning. You could have been so much more if you would have joined me. One day I will watch you die slowly one day before me. How long do you think you can keep your secret? I know everything about you and to make me whole I will embrace your great power – gift in time.'

She screams, 'It will all be mine! The stars the universe, everything and nothing will stand in my way!'

John, 'You're insane you need help Stacey… What happened to you, what happened that you became this way?'

Stacey, 'Nothing happened to me John, it's just we're two sides of the same coin. You're good and I am evil. This way I will be a God.'

John, 'By killing innocent people…?'

Stacey, 'We all have our dark side. I gave you the chance to join me but you went off with that bitch Kate Anderson… No one refuses me! Evil will always outshine good John. I am going to enjoy watching you suffer and when you least expect it, I will take everything that is close to you and burn it before your eyes. As much as I would love to chat I really must be going…worlds and mini universes to destroy if you get my drift. See you around my dear.

With that a teleport gate appears and before Stacey enters it she turns around and blows John a kiss and then with a laugh she enters the teleport gate and disappears…

John, 'For a while now I haven't heard a thing about Stacey Cannon. I suspect she is out there somewhere, making trouble. All I know is that somehow she has become very powerful and more insane than ever.

John thinks for a moment… A troubled expression upon his face…

'I read once in a book I was reading that if you were to enter the mind of the Devil you would carry the soul of Lucifer within you. Sometimes I think that Stacey Cannon has the soul of pure evil within her and God forbid anyone who tries to stand in her way...'

John finishes speaking and yawns. He smiles at Rogue with a sleepy smile.

John, 'Well as much as I would love to tell you more about my adventures or misadventures I think I should stop worrying about Kate. I am sure she can look after herself she has proved many times before. And I think I will turn in and get some sleep for a few hours. Good night Rogue.'

Rogue, 'Good night Master Parker.'

ARYAN RESEARCH BUREAU. DAY.

The house that Kate is in looks reassuringly normal. It is a solid old-fashioned building, spotlessly clean.

Kate speaks to the man as she follows him down the hall.

Kate, 'So what do I call you?'

Man, 'I am known just as the Caretaker. I'll show you the visitor's library.'

The visitor's library is a huge, incredibly silent room, thickly carpeted and lined with glass-fronted bookcases. There are displays cases of ancient documents scatted about the room.

Caretaker, 'There you are young lady. One of the finest collections of Aryan folk material in the country...'

Kate forces a smile and tries to hide her disgust.

Kate, 'I am sure it is.'

The man moves closer putting on the thick pebble glasses again and staring deep into her eyes.

Caretaker, 'Tell me about your partner.'

Kate, 'Sorry, I don't know what you mean.'

Caretaker, 'John Parker, how much does he know and what is he doing here in Germany?'

The pale eyes, magnified and distorted by the thick lenses stare into Kate's eyes and the questions become more insistent.

Caretaker, 'Tell me! You must answer... Why is John Parker here?'

Kate can feel the pressure of the Caretaker's mind battering at her own.

Kate snaps sharply, 'Aren't you being rather rude? If you are so curious about John you can talk to him yourself. I'm sure he'll be visiting you very soon.'

With a gasp the Caretaker steps back. He takes off his glasses and rubs his hand over his eyes.

Caretaker, 'Please forgive me. I have heard so much about Mr. Parker you see I am naturally curious. Please feel free to look around. I must get on with my work.'

With that he positively shoots out of the room.

Kate to herself, 'The little creep was trying to hypnotise me, so John was right they are up to something here'.

Kate starts to look around. But she finds nothing but old books. Suddenly she hears voices outside the doorway, she runs to the doorway and listens. The Caretaker is talking to someone down the hall.

Caretaker, 'She's here now. No he's not with her. Just the girl...'

Voice, 'And what has she told you?'

Caretaker, ''Nothing. I tried but even with mind amplifier... She has a strong will. Did you see the Fuehrer?'

Voice, 'Yes. Everyday he becomes more and more in our power.'

Kate hears the footsteps move closer to the door. Kate hurriedly moves away from the door. She sits down beside a table and starts leafing through a look. The footsteps come closer and closer and at last an extraordinary figure shuffles in the room. It is a tall, white haired, white bearded old man. He is muffled from head to toe in a voluminous cape. He moves quickly but somehow painfully too with the aid of a silver- headed scuttling along with an odd spider-like gait.

Kaiser, 'How do you do my dear? I am Doctor Kaiser.'

He has a deep melodious voice that of a much younger man. Kate stares at him for a moment.

'You are wondering about the reason for my somewhat extraordinary appearance? It is due to a misfortune I suffered at birth or rather at rebirth.'

Kate, 'I'm sorry.'

Kaiser, 'Well this is a most unexpected pleasure. Indeed I am only sorry John can't be with us here in person. Unfortunately Mr. Parker seems to dropped out of sight for quite a while now.'

Kate, 'I expect he'll pop up. He usually does.'

Kaiser, 'He does indeed. Sometimes with the most disconcerting results.'

Kate, 'You sound as if you know him.'

Kaiser, 'We met once long ago and far away. In a sense I owe my present condition to Mr. John Parker. I can't tell you much I look forward to our reunion.'

Kate looks at him oddly.

Kate, 'But you said it had happen at birth…'

Kaiser corrects her gently…

Kaiser, 'At rebirth...'

Kaiser glances around at the books in the library.

'Tell me my dear, what do you think of our little library here?'

Kate smiles.

Kate angrily, 'Well I ought to say something vague and tactful but I think it's the biggest load of rubbish I have ever seen. Dangerous rubbish that poisons people's minds.'

The Caretaker, who had just followed Kaiser into the room, looks shocked. Kaiser on the other hand seems amused by Kate's angry reply.

Kaiser, 'I couldn't agree more. Absolute rubbish- bolstered up by ludicrous filth scholarship. Aryan blood indeed! Their precious Aryan race doesn't even exist- it's a myth. And even if it did would it matter? What's the point trying to prove that one breed of human is better than another? It's like trying to prove that a flea is more pure- blooded than a louse.'

Kate, 'Then why bother with all this?'

Kaiser, 'I am afraid it's what the public wants.'

Kate, 'What public?'

Kaiser, 'The public-, which consists, largely I'm afraid of Reichsfuehrer, Heinrich Himmler and his merry men of the SS. Himmler has an endless interest in all this racial mumbo jumbo and in every other kind of mumbo jumbo come to that. Spiritualism old Teutonic folk myths, divination by pendulum- swinging, astrology… You name it and little Heinrich will pay a fortune to investigate it.'

Kate, 'You're not trying to tell me you're just in it for the money?'

Kaiser, 'You're right my dear the money is useful but it's not my prime motive.'

Kate, 'Then what is it?'

Kaiser, 'Oh influence shall we say instead?'

Kate, 'You mean power…'

Kaiser, 'If you like. Himmler is a gullible fool but he's the most powerful man in the Third Reich.'

Kate, 'Except for Hitler.'

Kaiser, 'Yes, indeed. But enough chit- chat… Let's get to Mr. Parker. You're sure you don't know where he is?'

Kaiser and Caretaker move closer towards her in a menacing way.

Nervously Kate starts to edge towards the door.

Kate, 'No, I don't. Thank you for your time gentlemen. I think I'd better go and look for him.'

With spider-like speed Kaiser moves to block her way.

Kaiser creepily, 'No, don't do that my dear. I've a better idea.'

Kate nervously, 'Oh yes? And what would that be?'

Kaiser, 'Simply stay with us. John's bound to come and find you in time…'

Kate shakes her head.

Kate, 'I like my idea better.'

Kaiser softly, 'But I don't…'

Kate, 'Please step out of the way I don't want to hurt you. I am leaving right now.'

Kaiser raises his silver- headed cane. Kate sees that the tip is glowing bright red like the top of a giant lit- cigar. He points the cane at a table and a laser bolt fires from the cane and blows a hole in the table where Kate sat beside earlier.

Kaiser looks at Kate proudly.

Kaiser, 'Do you like my weapon?' *Thinks for a moment then giggles.*

'That sounds rather rude doesn't it? Anyway it's a fairly simple piece of
laser technology. Your partner first encountered it in December 31st 1999.
It's been a long time for me but perhaps rather less for you?
Please don't move my dear. I'd far rather keep you in one piece at least till
John arrives. I've waited such a long time for this moment. I hope you
understand my dear.'

*Kate makes a dash for the door but Kaiser hits the back of Kate's head with
the cane and knocks her out into darkness.*

THE CASTLE OF THE BROTHERS OF THE APOCALYPSE

THE CASTLE OF THE BROTHERS OF THE APOCALYPSE. NIGHT.

*We see a giant gothic castle with a huge tower. It is a forbidding sight.
There is an air of evil about it and the huge dark clouds that hover over it in
this scene adds to the effect of an unspeakable evil about the place.*

CASTLE. NIGHT.

*Kate wakes in darkness. She tries to move and finds her horror that she is
fastened upright in a T – Shape by manacles at her wrists and ankles.*

*There is a sudden blaze of light. Burning torches are held close to her face,
and in their flicking light, she sees sinister black – robed, black – hooded
forms grouped around her in a semi – circle. They fall back to reveal an
even more awful and ghastly figure, a black – robed Priest in a hideous goat
mask. He carries an enormous ceremonial knife with a huge curved blade;
he starts stalking towards her Kate.*

*The razor – edged blade touches Kate's throat and she feels the string, as it
draws blood. She screams the place down and faints away.*

INVIDIOUS. JOHN'S ROOM.

John is asleep in his room aboard the Invidious...and is in a grip of a nightmare.

JOHN"S NIGHTMARE.

John is in a white room. A table before him...in the centre of the table rests a crystal – ball. He picks up the crystal ball he leans over it and stares deep into its cloudy depths. Suddenly a picture begins to form...

...It's Kate. She is chained to a wall in some kind of dungeon, surrounded by black – robed figures. She is menaced by a hideously masked figure holding a knife to her throat.

We see a close – up of the knife touching Kate's throat, we see a thin line of blood, and Kate screaming. The image fades...

John stands very, very still looking into the crystal ball and its cloudy depths. After a moment or two...the same image that John had seen before of Kate in terror...reappears with in the ball...The image fades and returns...the little sequence playing over and over again in a loop...

John can take no more and snatches up the crystal ball, he hurls it away screaming...

John, 'All right, all right. I get the bloody message.'

The white rooms fills with the awful sound of Kate screaming and the crystal ball explodes into a million tiny pieces...

INVIDIOUS. JOHN"S ROOM.

John wakes up with a scream and sits upright in his bed. He gets up and rushes from the room.

CASTLE. NIGHT.

Kate awakes in a largish room, more or less triangular except the outer wall, which has a window; this part of the room is curved. The walls are made of stone but some effort has been made to make the place comfortable. There are brightly coloured heraldic shields on the walls for rugs more furs strewn on chairs and couches.

Kate goes over to the window, which is open but barred and looks out. Ahead and below is a wide vista of rolling wooded countryside.

We hear faint shouting coming from directly below the window. Kate cranes her neck to look out and down. In the courtyard below a squad of muscular blond young men who are stripped to the waist and are going through complicated series of exercises under the shouted orders of an instructor.

Kate to herself, 'Just my luck... The place is full of bare-chested blond hunks and I'm locked up here. At least I suppose I'm locked in...'

Kate goes to a massive door and tries to open it. To her astonishment it opens. She finds herself on a wide stone staircase, which winds down to an enormous circular chamber a vast stone hall divided into different areas. Kate stands at the top of the stairs studying the busy scene below her. It is an amazing complex sight.

All kinds of different activities are going on simultaneously in different sections.

One area holds weapons from every era of Earth's past and future everything from handguns to machine guns and crossbows. Elsewhere black uniformed SS men are stripping and cleaning an assortment of weapons.

There is what looks like a high- tech medical area where machines hum and buzz. In this section are still more SS men lay rigidly to attention on simple military coats, which radiate the spokes of a wheel from a vast central console.

The men lay head- inwards and each man wares a oddly designed helmet linked to electronic cables to consoles. Even as Kate watches the men moving as one take the helmets from their heads swing their legs from the cots and stand to attention.

A second group of men are taking their place even as the first group form a squad and march away.

In the centre of the room is an open- plan control centre. It's illuminated screens show maps of Germany, of Europe, of Africa of Asia- in fact Kate sees of the entire world.

Standing in front of the map of Europe is Kaiser.

Beside is the sneering Caretaker is the Aryan Research Master. He wares a strange black uniform with a high- collared jacket. His bearing is now that of a soldier rather than a scholar. He glances briefly at Kate and then goes back to study the maps making marks on the screen with some sort of light pen.

Kaiser looks up as Kate comes down the stairs and crosses the hall towards him.

Kaiser, 'Ah, there you are… I trust you are rested. Are your quarters comfortable?'

Kate, 'They are now. When I first woke up I was in some kind of dungeon, surrounded by a bunch of creepy losers. Unless it was more than just a nightmare – '

Kate breaks off talking and with a gasp she catches a sight on one of the monitor screens. On it she sees herself in the image that John saw in the crystal ball in his nightmare abroad the Invidious. She sees herself scream in terror over and over again.

The sequence is repeated in a loop.

Kate with shock and horror, 'What the hell?'

Kaiser smiling, 'You might call it a trailer my dear. As they say in the cinema, a preview of coming attractions. It was recorded for the benefit of your friend John Parker.'

Kaiser flicks a switch and the picture changes to a close up of John leaning forward peering in tenthly at something.

Kaiser, 'He is having a dream a nightmare. Sent through one of our psychics. A kind of message if you will... Very soon he will have to take action.'

Kate, 'What kind of action?'

Kaiser, 'He will come here to find you. To save you if he can…'

Kate, 'Where's here?'

Kaiser, 'You are in the castle of 'The Brothers of the Apocalypse' my dear, hundreds of miles in the middle of nowhere. Himmler purchased this castle in person for the use of the SS. The Dark Tower where we are now was reserved for the members of the Reckoning Movement and the inner elite, the psychic shock troops of the SS…'

Kate looks around in a bored manner.

Kate, 'All this hi- tech equipment it's not from any future era I know it's not from here on Earth, is it? Are you from another world, other dimension?'

Kaiser, proudly, 'We hail from a dimension that exists alongside your own existence. We worked for the Reckoning Movement for over a millennium. We are creatures of the Dark Dimension…'

Kate glances at the monitor, which displays John. Suddenly the picture fragment breaks up, John's face vanishes and the screen goes blank.

Caretaker, ''He's broken the psychic link to his mind…'

Kaiser chuckles, 'Ah, John grows impatient. It won't be long…'

Kate, 'What are you talking about? You said we were hundreds of miles from anywhere? John doesn't even know where I am let alone know how to get here…'

Kaiser, 'The answer to all your questions are simple. John has a very powerful psychic mind and other powerful paranormal gifts too I suspect, as I have been witness to myself in 1999. He will find us. I have great faith in his ingenuity. He will find the way. Of course we mustn't make it too easy for him. That would spoil all the fun.'

The picture loop of Kate in the dungeon replaces that of John's face on the screen she glances at it for a moment, and then turns away in disgust.

Kate, 'I don't think much of your idea of fun. Are you telling me you staged all that nasty business in the dungeon just to make John think I was in danger?'

Kaiser, 'We recorded it to distress him but I'm afraid you really are in danger. The act of choosing is only a preliminary but it is still an important ceremony in its own right.'

Kate nervously, 'What do you mean, ceremony?'

Kaiser, 'Exactly what I say my dear. The unholy Priest – in this instance myself- inspects the Chosen One and if all goes well finds her acceptable. And then with the token of a knife the unholy Priest takes a first taste of the victim's blood.'

Kate touches her finger to her neck. To her horror she feels a tiny scar with dried blood.

Kate, 'You said a preliminary ceremony? Preliminary to what?'

Kaiser, 'To the Great Sacrifice of course... A Ceremony of Dedication to the Gods of the Apocalypse as they are known in my dimension… You my dear are to be the traditional Virgin Sacrifice I do hope you are qualified? '

Kate to her disgust finds herself blushing a furious red. Kaiser waves dismissively.

Kaiser, 'It really doesn't matter we certainly won't let a mere technicality stand in our way.

The whole thing is nonsense anyway to be honest; I made most of the sacred rituals up centuries ago in my dimension to keep certain members of our race under our power. Fear my dear brings about control and better still it impresses the cronies and that's what matters.'

Kate can do nothing but stare in horror at what Kaiser has said. Kaiser smiles at her and glances at the night sky through one of the arrow slits in the wall of the tower.

Kaiser gently, 'Time is getting on. I do hope John Parker won't be too long I'd hate him to miss your big moment.'

INVIDIOUS. IN EARTH'S ORBIT

The Invidious sits majestically just beyond Earth's orbit.

INVIDIOUS CONTROL ROOM.

John hurries into the control room. Rogue lets out a series of beeps and speaks...

Rogue, 'I take it from the grave expression upon your face that Miss Anderson is in danger Master Parker? '

John, 'The bastards sent me a psychic dream loop it took me a while to pinpoint where she's being held. Listen carefully Rogue and please try not to malfunction this time, Kate's life may depend on it, okay?'

Rogue, 'I will perform perfectly sir. Better than perfectly... As Miss Anderson is in danger...Master Parker.'

John, 'that's good enough for me old friend. Now before I go, I want you to listen very, very carefully...and do as I say to the letter.'

KAISER'S CASTLE TOWER. NIGHT.

The teleport gate appears at the top of a staircase. John looks down at the control room below.

John to himself, 'An impressive set-up…'

He looks on the scene below lost in thought. Suddenly he hears a voice in his mind, the voice of Kaiser.

Kaiser, 'John Parker, I sense you are here. Make your way to the main chamber of the Dark Tower. But hurry John! Your young friend or should I say lover is here and she will soon be in some distress. Make haste if you want to arrive while she is still alive.'

John sees a bustle of activity in the centre of the room below. Then he notices Kate. She is being strapped to a wooden trestle table and the table is upended against a store pillar.

Kaiser stands before the pillar his silver- topped cane in his hands. He twists the knob of the cane and the tip glows red. He slashes the cane towards the table in a diagonal motion and the top left- hand corner of the table falls away. Kaiser then shows off the right- hand corner.

He pauses…

Kaiser, 'You see the principle John? My laser- cane is a precision instrument but the risk to you to your friend is constantly increasing. If I miscalculate she may lose an ear or a finger even a hand or a foot. Don't worry she won't die. The wounds will cauterise themselves and I'll be sure to leave enough of her in one piece for our purposes.'

Kaiser swings the laser- cane in a high arc slicing a chunk off the top of the table and a tuft from Kate's hair in the process.

Kate screams, 'John! If you're there don't come out. He's just bluffing!'

Kaiser swings the cane in a low sweep cutting a slice off the bottom of the table and removing the toe of Kate's shoe in the act.

John starts to walk down the staircase calmly and across the hall with his hands in his pockets as if on a summer walk…

John, 'Enough of that behaviour! Show's over… I'm here!'

Every face in the hall turns toward him.

John walks over to Kate he takes out a pocket knife from his pocket and uses it to cut the straps that bound Kate to the mangled table.

Kate, 'Quite an entrance John… Don't worry they can't scare me.'

With that Kate faints into John's arms.

KAISER'S CASTLE. NIGHT.

John and Kate are confident in the luxurious quarters where Kate had awakened for the second time.

John, 'Well the door is locked and there's an SS guard outside as well. I can't believe they took my pocket knife I've had that knife since I was a child...'

Kate, 'Never mind that.'

Pauses

'Honest John me screaming and fainting...'

John, 'You've got to stop clinging to this macho image. In your place I'd have been screaming the place down ages ago...'

Kate, 'Well you're not me... I hope you've got something up your sleeves...'

John, 'Several something's actually. Remember Kate whatever you do react naturally...'

The guard outside the door unlocks it and Kaiser walks in.

John, 'Come for a good gloat? It's the usual procedure in these situations.'

Kaiser studies John from the doorway.

Kaiser, 'So you've got a little older John. Happens to all of us in the end. But all in all you haven't changed that much. You were an insignificant man when we met and you still are...'

John, 'I may not have changed much but you have. At lest if you really are who you say you are. Used to be tall, dark and handsome didn't you? I heard you'd been killed- though come to think of it I never checked to see if you were alive or not after what happened...'

Kaiser, 'If you remember I was shot John. But not killed. Shot several times at close range with energy weapons. Would you care to know how I survived?'

John, 'I've a feeling you're going to tell me...'

Kaiser, 'after you had left the Enigma Federation troopers came across my body they were about to dispose of it. When they realized I was still alive. Just barely but alive... You know how amazingly tough we trans-dimensional beings are John.'

John, 'I know about you're races amazing regeneration powers if that's what you mean? But anyway, do carry on...'

Kaiser, 'They called one of their scientists and he was so amazed he ordered me sent to a Enigma Federation base on Mars- things had been cleared up here on Earth by you. So I was sent to Mars without you knowing.'

John, 'Why did they bother with you? From what I remember and the trouble you caused the Enigma Federation would have been glad to have you dead.'

Kaiser, 'Oh there was no thought of curing me I assure you John. They just wanted to see how long it would take me to die. They threw me in the ships hold and on the journey to Mars I started to regenerate. However because of my massive injuries the extensive tissue damage the complete tact of all medical care the...'

Pause

'...The regeneration aborted...'

Kate notices the pain on John's face. He seems to have been taken back by what Kaiser has just told him.

John, 'Oh God, the regeneration aborted...'

Kaiser, 'Would you like to see what an aborted regeneration looks like John?'

With that Kaiser throws back his cape and for a moment John and Kate get a glimpse of a malformed bandaged- swathed torso sprouting twisted limbs- stubby extra limbs...

It is though two bodies have been clumsily joined together. Kate turns away in horror.

Kaiser, 'I will leave you to image the state of the skull.'

Kaiser starts wagging his huge oddly shaped head.

Kaiser, 'As you see I conceal it as best as I can.'

John, 'I hear the Enigma Federation is doing research into tissue regeneration. It's supposed to be very advanced. Maybe they could help you with regeneration therapy.'

Kaiser, 'laughs, 'At this stage John? I doubt it. Besides what if they could? They would cure me- and then sentence me to death or rather in my case temporal dissolution. Un- being which is worse than death…'

John suddenly, 'Which reminds me… That follow I caught a glimpse of out there. High- collared black uniform and built- in sneer…'

Kate, 'Yes I saw him too. He was the Caretaker at the Aryan Research Centre.'

John, 'Now he really was sentenced to temporal dissolution. What's more I saw the sentence carried out. Which was fine by me the man was a monster…'

Kaiser, 'The sentence you saw carried out was upon his father. The person you saw is his son his successor. There is a strong family resemblance. Like me he has no reason to love the Enigma Federation- or humans for that matter.'

John, 'Well, it's all very nice sitting here chatting about the good old days. But it doesn't explain what you're doing here and now.'

Kaiser, 'Gaining my revenge on you John.'

John, 'I don't follow.'

Kaiser, 'I survived as a medical curiosity. However I came to the attention of the Reckoning Movement to them I had become like a God- like- figure. They believe in my plan for Armageddon and from such a apocalypse a new race would arise. A master race from the ashes of the old… They helped me escape from the Enigma Federation. And all they asked me was to carry out what you once stopped me from doing.

Very soon there will be a master race in charge of this planet and I shall rule as a God. And in doing this I will also have my revenge on you for the shame of defeat you inflicted on me in 1999. But I have plans…'

Kate cutting in, 'Now I suppose we're going to hear all about that too?'

Kaiser turns away as if to leave the room.

Kaiser, 'I intended to show you something of our operation here- but as you please... You have long hours before you and little to do with them. But if you prefer to stare at the walls until it is time to die...'

John hurriedly, 'No, no... Come on Kate lets not be ungracious. There's nothing to read and the telly's hardly been invented yet and satellite is decades away, we may as well take the tour. Remember knowledge is always useful.'

Kaiser raps on the door and the outside guard unlocks it. John and Kate follow him out.

Kaiser leads John and Kate down some stairs and across the main hall to a control centre where the Caretaker is stood brooding before map screens.

Kaiser, 'I have brought our guests Caretaker. I thought it might amuse you to explain our plans for the final conquest of Earth- and then the galaxy.'

Caretaker, 'This is a great pleasure Mr. Parker. I have been waiting for a long time for a chance to meet you and to repay my debt.'

John, 'Don't think of it as a debt. Spoiling your fathers' evil schemes was a pleasure.'

Caretaker, coldly, 'The basic ides of that first plan the one you interfered with Mr. Parker was as you know was for us trans- dimensional beings to take over the minds of the most powerful humans in charge of you're world. However we didn't know how strong willed some of you humans are. And when you got involved things got how I should say a little over complex. From what I've heard you have many gifts one of which being a powerful psychic mind. But our first plan wasn't really thought out enough.'

John, 'Let's be honest. It was an insane plan a dogs' breakfast of a plan. It was starting to go wrong even before you turned up.'

Caretaker, 'There were certain problems. The difficulty of brainwashing ans taking over the minds of so many men and women the consequent Enigma Federation resistance in different time zones. '

John, 'Precisely. A dogs' breakfast...'

Caretaker, 'However my kind are still convinced that Earth is perfect for breeding a new powerful master race which the Dark Dimension along side the Reckoning Movement shall rule. After the great Apocalypse the human race will reform into a race of killers, which will be used to take over galaxy after galaxy. Humans have the best characteristics to form such a new master race.So we made use of the time- scanning equipment provided by the Reckoning Movement to study Earths history and we found- all this!'

The Caretaker makes a sweeping gesture and indicates the ranks of SS men the swastika banners on the wall.

Caretaker, 'A nation a government dedicated to some end as the Dark Dimension and the Reckoning Movement. And with that nation a chosen elite even more dedicated than the rest. Most of our work was done for us already.'

John nods.

John, 'I see what you mean. Unquestioning obedience total ruthlessness naked aggression- this lot are very much like robots already.'

Kaiser, 'Exactly. Do you realize John that these men all undergo two years of brutal training before they are permitted to call themselves members of the SS? When we take them over they are preconditioned through genetic-engineering and a form of mind control. A few adjustments really… And the process is complete.'

Kaiser raises his voice.

'You there!'

One of the blond giant SS men doubles across and comes to attention. He is totally expressionless. The man is no longer human.

Kaiser, 'There is so little humanity left in them when we take them over it is a simple matter to remove the rest.'

Kaiser looking up at the giant towering before him he snaps.

Kaiser, 'Helmet grenade.'

The blond giant marches over to an alcove set in the tower wall next to the weapons section. At a gesture from Kaiser they all follow. They watch the SS man take a steel helmet from a rack and put it on and select a grenade from a wooden crate.
Then he steps into the alcove. A thick transparent shield slides across the front.

Caretaker, 'Watch closely.'

The Caretaker nods to the SS man. Unbelievingly John and Kate see the man pulls the pin from the grenade balance the grenade on his helmet and stand to attention. Seconds later there is a muffled explosion and the alcove fills with smoke.

The shield slides back the smoke clears and there is the SS man. The helmet mangled by the blast blood trickles from the man's nose and ears. But still he stands rigidly to attention blue eyes staring blankly ahead.

John, 'Quite a party trick...'

Kaiser laughs, 'Believe it or not that is a standard SS training exercise. But for us he would do it without the helmet. Would you like to see John? I assure you he would obey.'

John hurriedly, 'No, No I'll take your word for it. I am sure he is a very obedient pat.'

Kaiser, 'Medical section.'

The SS man marches away. Kaiser leads the group back to the control area.

Kaiser, 'They do not fear pain or death anymore as you can see.'

John, 'Well, why should they? After all they're not really alive. So what do you plan to do with your zombie army?'

Kaiser taps the map.

Kaiser, 'We shall rewrite Earth's history John. First we shall ensure that Hitler wins this war.'

John, 'And how do you propose to do that?'

Kaiser, 'Adolf Hitler is a flawed genius. A man with great talents- and with enormous weaknesses... We have accentuated the talents.'

John, 'By boosting the powers of persuasion and charisma?'

Kaiser, 'Hitler has an extraordinary power to arouse raw emotion in a crowd. If that power is boosted- the technology to do this is relatively simple John- the results are quite amazing...'

Kaiser lifts a small complex- looking piece of equipment from the table.

Kaiser, 'With this and me sitting in close range to Hitler I am able to boost his natural powers. All by wearing this simple telepathic amplifier...'

He smiles wryly.

'My cape can cover more than my deformities when necessary.'

Caretaker, 'We shall also correct the disastrous errors of judgement. France will be over run just as before but this time there will be no fatal delays in following up the victory Britain will be swiftly over whelmed as well.'

John, 'What about America?'

Caretaker, 'If England is conquered quickly America will accept the fact. There is a strong isolationist party there as it is.'

John, 'And Russia?'

Kaiser, 'The treaty will be kept. There will be no attack on Russia, not yet. That was the second mistake. We consolidate our grip on the continent. We move carefully one step at a time, Asia, Africa, the Far East. We provoke war between Russia and America so the two giants destroy each other John but we shall breed a new master race from its ends. We shall achieve our goal- a Nazi Earth- controlled by the Reckoning Movement and the Dark Dimension.
And even that is only the first step. We shall force the pace of Earths scientific development- atomic weapons a star drive a space fleet. When we are ready we will also destroy your great Enigma Federation then we will conquer the galaxy!'

Caretaker, 'A Nazi galaxy... In time a Nazi universe.'

John, 'A Reckoning Movement and Dark Dimension universe more like. With you lot pulling the strings God help us. How do you plan to make this insane idea work exactly?'

Kaiser, 'That is not finally decided. The most obvious way was to work through the man Hitler. He has remarkable powers. He is the focal point of the whole regime.
But he has become strangely unreliable and we are finding it harder and harder to control him. We fear a complete breakdown.'

John, 'Won't that put a crimp in your plans?'

Kaiser, 'Not at all... We shall simply replace him with Himmler. Since he already controls the SS it will be even simpler.'

Kate, 'And Goering?'

Kaiser, 'Too individualistic...'

Pause

'He will be disposed of.'

Kate, 'How much does Himmler know about all this?'

She gestures around her.

'The mind control... the brainwashing... all this hi- tech stuff?'

Kaiser, 'Very little... He accepts this tower as a sort of inner sanctum and stays away. He prefers to think of our assistance as being super- natural rather than scientific. I have more to show you John. Excuse us Caretaker.'

The Caretaker nods dismissively and goes back to his maps and screens. Kaiser leads John and Kate across the hall to the staircase, which continues downwards. With a gesture Kaiser summons two SS guards to follow them.'

Kaiser, 'Don't even think of escaping John. You are in a fortress within a fortress with guards everywhere. You have only the illusion of liberty'.

Kaiser pauses at a vaulted doorway of a huge chamber. He gives Kate a ghastly smile.

Kaiser, 'Our chapel my dear... This is a side entrance the main door is at the rear.'

John and Kate look through the doorway. The huge vaulted chamber is hung with swastika flags. High- backed stone seats each decorated with curved SS insignia and they are grouped in semi- circles around a great stone stab of an altar. There is a swastika banner behind the altar and a flanking pair of candleholders with huge black candles.

The altar is curved with strange esoteric runes. Kate sees with horror that its surface is dark with the stains of old blood.

Kaiser notices the direction of her gaze and laughs.

Kaiser, 'Chickens... One or two cats, the odd lamb... Tomorrow night will be our first attempt at the real thing so to speak. Since the war has finally begun. I felt something more impressive was more in order. We were going to use one of our young SS men but then you came along... '

Kate, 'Just my luck...'

Kaiser leads them from the chapel still further downwards to a point where the gloom of the staircase is replaced with a blaze of light. Opening a steel door Kaiser takes them into a small, brightly lit control room. There are rows of dials and switches and a glass window that looks out over a much larger area, a vast underground chamber filled with great gleaming metal tanks linked by walkways and gantries and overhead cranes.

It means nothing to Kate but John seems to recognize it. He looks at Kaiser genuine shock on his face.

John, 'That isn't...?'

Kaiser triumphantly, 'It is indeed. A fully automated atomic reactor... When we deem the time is right the Fuehrers primitive rockets will have nuclear warheads.'

John appalled, 'You'll destroy this planet!'

Kaiser, 'Maybe. But from the brimstone the new master race will arise our children of power. The children of Gods...'

John, 'Oh share me you lot are insane. Nothing good will come of this. Even you must know that.'

Kaiser, reassuringly, 'don't worry we'll only use the warheads on larger counties, Russia, China, America. They're big enough to soak up a bit of radiation. And there'll be no nuclear retaliation, remember no nuclear war as such.'

John, 'What makes you so sure?'

Kaiser, 'We shall be the only country with atomic weapons.'

With that Kaiser leads them to the door.

Kaiser, 'Well, John that concludes what you are pleased to call the tour. I think you should return to your quarters and rest. A trying time awaits you.'

CASTLE TOWER STAIRCASE. NIGHT.

*Flanked by the ever- present guards the group begin climbing the stairs.
Once John and Kate are back at the door to their quarters John speaks…*

John, 'You've made your plans for Kate abundantly clear. What about me?'

Kaiser turns from the door.

Kaiser, 'I am glad you asked John. Firstly you will attend tomorrow night's
ceremony and witness the death of someone you love. Then- you remember
the DDTS.'

Kate, 'What's DDTS?'

John, 'Dark Dimension Time Ships… Primitive time machines- with a
limited shelf life…'

Kaiser, 'That's an unkind but accurate description. After the ceremony we
shall require the location of your time ship what is it called now? The
Invidious isn't it? Once that is ours we can reproduce it conquer time as
well as space.'

John indignantly, 'Out of the question.'

Kaiser, 'Oh you will tell us John. We shall take your mind to pieces like a
watch. Of course one or two of the parts may get broken in the process- but
that really doesn't matter.'

John, 'It doesn't?'

Kaiser, 'Once I have wrested from it the secrets of your time ship your mind
will be of no further interest to me. But your body…'

John looking embarrassed

'Please, lady is present.'

Kaiser, 'We are both alike really John. We have both undergone genetic
engineering to improve our minds, since birth. Regeneration therapy may be
to late for me but our brains and our bodies are compatible. I'm sure my
scientists can manage a simple brain transplant.'

Kaiser studies John with detached clinical interest.

Kaiser, 'To be honest it isn't the body I would have chosen but it's infinitely
superior to the one I have. When all this is over John I shall be you- and you

or whatever shattered gibbering remnant of you is left will be me. Appropriate don't you think? A crippled mind in a crippled body…'

DARK CEREMONY

KAISER'S CASTLE. NIGHT.

John and Kate are talking in the locked room.

Kate, 'To be perfectly honest with you John there are one or two things about our present situation I'm not really crazy about.'

John, 'At least you're playing the leading lady. How would you like to be condemned to a bit part as Quasimodo, the Hunchback of the Reich?'

Kate, 'He's certainly got it in for you, hasn't he? Not only twisted but bitter we well.'

John, 'He used to be devilishly handsome fellow you see. He resents the change and thinks it's all my fault.'

Kate, 'And is it?'

John, 'Only in the sense I had to stop him last time. If I could have done things another way...'

They stop talking and stare at each other for a moment.

Kate, 'Are we going to get out of this John? Alive in one piece- and in our own bodies I mean?'

John sombrely, 'I hope so. But maybe not until the last minute… There's a lot more than just us at stake you see and I can't leave with the job undone. There may have to be… '

Kate cutting in, 'Sacrifices?'

John doesn't reply. After a moment…

Kate, 'When old nasty said I was someone you love was he right?'

John, 'Yes he was. And yes I do love you.'

Kate yawns and stretches out at the couch.

Kate, 'Better get some rest. I want to look my best tonight.'

She jokes trying to be brave.

'Just do whatever it takes to get the job done John. That's what counts.'

Kate closes her eyes and drifts off to sleep. John sits in his chair gazing out through the arrow slit at the dawn sky. Soon he too is asleep.

KAISER'S CASTLE. NIGHT.

John awakes and is shocked to find Kate gone. He runs to the door and starts to pound on it. Instantly the door swings open. There stands Kaiser, SS guards beside him. Kaiser is wearing a black robe with a black hood and he carries another on his arm.

Kaiser, 'Time to go John. It will be time soon.'

John, 'Where's Kate?'

Kaiser, 'She is being prepared. Don't worry you'll see her soon. Put this on John. Formal dress for the ceremony…'

John doesn't move. But he stands unresisting while at a gesture from Kaiser the SS guards put the robe on him, thrusting his arms in wide sleeves and pulling the hood over his head.

Kaiser, 'I hope you'll enjoy the ceremony. It's a bit of a hotchpotch I fear. I cobbled it up myself from the more colourful bits of Teutonic mythology. I trust the Reckoning Movement appreciates all my trouble.'

John, 'The Reckoning Movement is coming?'

Kaiser, 'Some of its members as there are some of my kind. This whole ceremony is largely for they're benefit. I just hope some of the cronies don't faint at the vital moment. Some of them are terribly squeamish hate the sight of blood.'

CASTLE COUNT YARD. NIGHT.

The main door of the tower is standing wide open revealing a hideous sight of evil.

Kaiser, 'We assemble in the count yard. Then we file in through the main entrance.'

The main count yard of the castle forms the background to a grim and terrifying scene. It is lined with black- uniformed SS guards bearing blazing torches. Their fiery light reveals a sinister procession forming up in the courtyard. There is something very unpleasant about the double line of black- robed, black- hooded figures n the flicking torchlight.

The procession sets off. Kaiser and John at the head.

CASTLE CHAPEL. NIGHT.

They file into the chapel and take their places filing up from the rear entrance filling up the rows of stone seats.

The black- hooded figures sit arms folded in solemn silence. The light from the blazing torches of the SS guards flicker on the swastika banners the heraldic shields and the dreadful bloodstained altar.

The sacrificial victim is brought in. They have dressed her in a flowing white robe and her hands are bound. She is staring straight ahead moving like a sleepwalker.

John whispering to himself, 'Drugged. Probably just as well...'

Kaiser stands beside Kate at the altar the shape of his twisted body visible even beneath the robes. On the altar before him lays a hideous goat mash and a huge ceremonial knife.

The ceremony begins...

John doesn't pay much attention. There is a great deal of chanting and intoning and long rambling players from Kaiser addressed to the spirits of the Ancient Masters and a weird variety of Gods.

The ceremony drones on hour after hour. Through the slit in the wall we see the sky grow lighter, Kaiser shouts...

Kaiser, 'A new dawn is almost upon us!'

At a command from Kaiser the torches are extinguished. They all wait in smoky darkness waiting for the dawn.

Kaiser gives another signal. Two black- hooded figures stretch Kate on the back of the altar her head projecting over the edge. Kaiser reaches for the mash and puts it on. He stretches out his hand for the knife.

Suddenly John leaps to his feet.

John shouting, 'No!'

The Caretaker looks up.

Caretaker, 'What is the meaning of this John Parker? You know there is nothing you can do.'

John passionately, 'I've been such a fool. I wish to join Kaiser and you in forming a new era. I have many skills to share. I wish to prove my total loyalty to the Reckoning Movement and the Dark Dimension. There on the altar is the woman I love the person I love most in the world. To Kaiser she is nothing. But if I sacrifice her to the dark Gods then the sacrifice will have true meaning. I beg you let me show my total loyalty.'

The Caretaker seems amused and also deeply moved.

Caretaker, 'I sense you are telling the truth. If you do what you say it will be a noble sentiment Mr. Parker. Very well perform the sacrifice!'

Kaiser makes no objection as John moves behind the altar. Kaiser speaks his voice a whisper, muffled by the hideous mask.

Kaiser, 'Will you go as far as this John to save your own skin?'

John, 'Try me.'

Kaiser, 'It won't work you know. All these games you're playing. Still go ahead. It's a delicious refinement- I only wish I'd thought of it myself.'

Kaiser hands John the knife.

Kaiser, 'Decapitation is the prescribed method if you hadn't guessed. And do try to get her head off in one stroke John. Nothing spoils a ceremony more than a lot inelegant hacking about.'

John takes the knife and looks down.

Kate's eyes gaze up at him her hair hanging down like a curtain.

Incredibly she smiles.

The ray of light from the rising sun strikes the altar.

The knife flashes down.

And severs Kate's bonds.

At the same time John's other hand reaches into his pocket and sweeps upward like a fast bowler hurtling some sort of object or device at the ceiling.

The explosion is shattering in the confined space and most of the chapel ceiling comes down showering the black- robed figures with dust and rubble.

John throws Kate over his shoulder and sprints out of the side door and up the stairs. He hasn't gone very far before he realizes Kate is kicking and struggling.

He puts her down takes her hand and starts pulling her up the stairs.

TOWER STAIRCASE. MORNING.

John, 'I thought you were drugged'.

Kate, 'I was just shamming scared stiff. Well to be honest I was scared stiff. I mean talk about leaving things to the last minute...'

An SS guard appears before them aiming a machine pistol. John springs at him like a tiger wrenches away the pistol and clouts him under the jaw with the butt. The SS man falls to the ground.

Kate, 'So much for the supermen give me that gun!'

John, 'Why?'

Kate, 'Because you're much too squeamish...'

Clocking the pistol Kate sprays a hail of bullets down the staircase to discourage pursuit.

Kate, 'Where to John?'

John, 'Up. All the way on the top...'

They met only one more guard all the way to the top and Kate shoots him down without a second thought.

John shouting, 'I hope you're not enjoying this too much.'

Kate, 'Just getting a bit of my own back John!'

. *KAISER'S CASTLE TOWER. DAY.*

John and Kate come out through the doorway on the top of the tower. John bars the doorway behind them.

Kate, 'That won't keep the massed Nazi hordes out for long will it?'

John goes to the parapet peers down towards the gates.

John, 'They'll have other things to worry about before very long. Come and look.'

Kate joins John at the parapet. A long straight road leads up to the castle gates and down it a column of dust is moving steadily towards them.

Kate, 'What is it? And who is it?'

John, 'the, what is an armoured column. The men unless I'm very much mistaken is Hermann Goering playing the part for this performance only of the US Cavalry.'

Kate, 'Why would he do that?'

John, 'I got Rogue to telephone him after I came to join you. I had Rogue to tell him that this castle was a hotbed of treason and that everyone from Himmler himself to Kaiser and his SS were plotting to knock him off.'

Kate, 'And you think he brought it?'

John, 'Why not? It's what he'd do to Himmler if he had the chance.'

The column is fast approaching the main gates. It consists of a row of jeep like vehicles, same of them mounted with guns all of them crammed with grey- clad soldiers. In the passenger front seat of the leading vehicle a corpulent figure in a sky- blue uniform is stood up in a commanding position.

John, 'There he is. Iron Fatty in person! Mind you at the moment he seems to think he's Rommel.'

They see Goering is arguing furiously with the SS sentries on the castle wall by the gate.

Kate, 'What's going on?'

The yard below them is full of black- uniformed and black- robed figures all milling about and asking the same question.

John, 'In this instance too much jaw, jaw and not enough war, war.'

JOHN

Pass me one of the shells from that rack would you Kate?

The little anti- aircraft gun is a fairly simple piece of machinery and it doesn't take John long to figure out how it works.

John, 'So if the shell goes in the loading chamber here and this is the firing lever here...'

There is a sudden explosion the gun bucks and recoils and a shell whistle over the head of the armoured column bursting on the other side.

John, 'A bit wild... Still it seems to have done the trick.'

The members of the armoured column scatter and take cover and are soon returning what they think is the enemy's fire. The SS sentries naturally shoot back and soon there is a fierce little battle raging.

John, 'Iron Fatty's not doing very well. He can't seem to get past the main gate.'

Kate, 'Maybe you should have sent for Rommel instead...'

John grins at Kate.

John, 'You know maybe you're right, maybe I should have...'

John starts fiddling with levers depressing the angle of the gun barrel. He sights along the barrel.

John, 'Ah, here we are. Shell please Kate. Load- Fire!'

Half of the castles front gate disappears blown away from the inside.

John, 'Quick another one, before they realize where it's coming from.'

A second shell takes out the rest of the gate and the armoured column roars through the gap all guns blazing. Battle is joined black uniforms against grey; there is furious fighting all around the courtyard.

John and Kate observe the battle from a high like spectators at a military match but in their little entertainment the bodies that fell down don't get up again. The conditioned SS men of Kaiser fight with fanatical energy quite careless of their own lives.

But the grey- clad troops of the regular army seem more than able to hold their own and very soon there are far less black uniforms than grey ones on the ground.

John, 'Those SS zombies of Kaiser's aren't doing at all well. They're so fearless they're easy to kill. A good soldier doesn't die for his country he gets the enemy to die for his.'

Kate, 'I thought you didn't approve of violence John?'

John, 'I don't, not usually. And if my head Priest from the Enigma Federation that taught me as a student saw me now he would have had a heart attack. Maybe I'm getting a bit of my own back too. Maybe I'm being corrupted. Time to go I think so I can think things through.'

Kate, 'How? In case you hadn't noticed we're on top of a tower surrounded by Nazi fanatics busily shooting at each other. I'm sure they'd be only too pleased to start shooting at us for a change.'

John doesn't seem to hear Kate something has caught his eye. He stares up at the sky.

John, 'Hang on. What's this?'

A light aeroplane is gliding down towards the castle. It touches down on a wide road by the gate and solitary brown uniformed figure gets out. The figure strides through the shattered gates and into the courtyard and everywhere the figure passes men stop fighting and come to attention hands raised in salute.

Suddenly the battle is over.

Kate, 'that's not who I think it is, is it?'

John, 'I'm afraid so. I don't like the look of this at all. Kate, come on.'

TOWER STAIRCASE. DAY.

They run down the stairs through the empty tower.

CASTLE COURTYARD. DAY.

They hide behind the ruins of the main gate and watch. The courtyard is littered with dead bodies and in the centre stand Goering and Himmler, arguing furiously- watched with benign amusement by a third man- Adolf Hitler.

Without warning John has a vision of the Caretaker going into some sort of high- tech chamber, there is a bright light, energy swells around inside the chamber...

The Caretaker screams out and then John has an image of Hitler, his eyes glowing with unearthly eerie silver light.

The vision ends and John stares at Kate with horror.

Kate, 'what is it John? What's the matter?'

John, 'The Caretaker has transformed himself into pure energy matter; he must have done it while everybody was busy fighting among themselves in battle... '

Kate looks confused.

Kate, 'So what are you saying?'

John, 'He has taken over the mind of Hitler possessed him if you prefer, like a demon possessing an innocent soul. With the Caretaker in control of Hitler's mind he'll feed him enough knowledge and power to be almost like a mini- God.'

John and Kate watch as Hitler leads the troops and men back to their vehicles. Soon every one has left. After everyone has left John thinks for a moment looking incredibly worried and turns to Kate.

John, 'We have to do something. We better get to the Invidious so I can think things out.'

Kate, 'I agree.'

John fishes in his pocket and he looks at Kate with a stricken face.

John, 'Well, that's just great… Talk about having a bad day…'

Kate sighs.

Kate, 'What now?'

John looks at Kate like a child that has been caught steeling.

John, 'I seem to have lost my teleport key.'

Before Kate can answer a hideous voice speaks from somewhere…

Voice, 'That need not trouble you John Parker. For you the world ends now.'

John and Kate stare at the direction where the voice is coming from and watch in horror as a black shape rises out of the mud. It is Kaiser. His cape is drenched with blood.

The dead SS corpses also start to lurch to their feet.

Kaiser leans heavily on his cane.

He gives John and Kate a ghastly smile.

Kaiser, 'You know the Old Prussian army had a favourite expression. Corpse discipline. The kind of discipline that makes a corpses jump to attention. As you see John I have achieved it. '

John looks around at the semi- circle of men- dead men. Their blue eyes are blanker than usual, the bloodstained bullet riddled bodies bare terrible wounds. Yet still they stand and move and obey orders.

Kaiser, 'Corpse discipline John. They are the elite of my elite. Complete mental linkage…They are sustained by my will. While I live they cannot die.
Once again you have turned up to ruin my plans John Parker. Soon too I shall die. But not before I have seen you and your beautiful companion turn to pieces.'

The army of corpses begin lurching towards John and Kate.

John, 'Quick Kate, the tower…'

They sprint across the courtyard and duck inside. Kate helps John to close the great door and drop the locking bar.

CASTLE AT THE BASE OF TOWER STAIRCASE. DAY.

John, 'Wait here for me. And hold them off whatever you do.'

Kate, 'How? Its no use shooting them they're already dead!'

John, 'Try grenades.'

John disappears down the stairs. Kate remembers the grenade- on- helmet demonstration. She rushes over to the arms section finds the grenade box and lugs it across the floor to a position near the base of the staircase. Kate notices a smoking line moving up from the bottom of the door. It moves up across and down again tracing the shape of a small door with the larger one.

Kate, 'Kaiser's laser cane, doesn't that man know when to call it a day?'

When Kaiser has finished cutting, the door is kicked from the outside and falls inwards. A black shape blocks the hole; Kate pulls the pin on the first grenade and throws it through.

The explosion blows the black shape away but another takes its place.

Kate loses count of the number of times the sequence is repeated. Soon the number of grenades in the box in getting low... As the dead SS men lurch towards her she grabs the last few grenades and retreats towards the stairs. They are all through now Kaiser as well. He smiles and raises his cane, Kate throws the last grenade and something grabs her arm...

It's John.

John, 'Come on up to the top!'

. TOWER STAIRCASE. DAY.

Kate races up the stone staircase after John trying to block out the sound of the dragging feet behind her.

Kate, 'What's going on John?'

John, 'They're got an atomic reactor down in the basement. Can't leave that sort of thing lying around in the late thirties. Far too anachronistic...'

Kaiser, 'So what did you do?'

As if in answer to her question the whole tower starts to shudder.

John, 'Threw it into overload...'

Kate, 'How long have we got?'

John opens the door to the top of the tower.

. *CASTLE TOWER. DAY.*

John, 'Well it's hard to be precise, it's a very primitive installation. But judging by the sounds its making- not... very... long!'

He hauls Kate out onto the roof of the tower. Suddenly she realizes the full horror of the situation.

Kate, 'Hold it John! We're being chased to the top of the tower by Nazi zombies- and your solution is top blow the tower up with an atomic bomb?'

John, 'That's right. It seemed a pretty neat idea at that time. What's wrong?'

The whole tower seems to be swaying. Huge cracks appear in the parapet and a chunk falls off.

Kate, 'John! We are standing on the top of the tower. The one you are blowing up!'

John, 'Not for long...'

John produces a device from one of his pocket, the device looks like a key ring he presses a control.

Nothing happens.

John looks worried.

A huge crack appears in the stone roof of the tower and some bits of the parapet fall off. A deep rumble fills the air; the whole tower is lashing to and fro like a ship's mast in a gale.

Kate, 'Well John?'

John frowns thoughtfully. He shakes the key ring, still nothing happens. In disgust he throws the thing away. He thinks for a moment, then grins and puts his fingers in his mouth; he gives out a piercing whistle.

The Invidious materializes in midair hovering about three feet above the edge of the tower.

John, 'Blast. It's always the little things.'

He takes out something that looks like a small credit card from his pocket.

'Give me a leg up Kate!'

Kate bends down, John puts his feet on her shoulders and she slowly straightens up. John reaches out for a control panel of the hull of the Invidious. The ground ripples under Kate's feet. Kate staggers and John falls against the floating time ship.

John, 'Keep still woman!'

Kate tries but it's like doing a balancing act on a trampoline. John somehow manages to use the small credit card like object to swipe a slot in a control panel on the hull of the Invidious.

A large hatchway opens and he scrambles inside. He stands in the open hatchway reaching down with his hand to get Kate.

She can't quite reach his outstretched hand.

Kate, 'I can't do it John. You'll have to go without me!'

John, 'shouting, 'Jump!'

He leans out the hatchway at a dangerous angle.

'Just grab my hand!'

Kate, 'I tell you I can't...'

Suddenly the door to the tower opens. It is Kaiser, zombie soldiers behind him. Kate leaps in the air like a terrified kangaroo. John grabs her wrist hauling her up and through the hatchway with amazing ease.

John, shouts, 'Close the hatchway quickly Kate!'

Kate turns to close the hatchway and catches a glimpse of Kaiser emerging from the tower door. The vibration of the tower triggers off some conventional explosives... Suddenly a great tongue of fire belches out from the doorway, engulfing Kaiser. There bathed in the flame Kate sees just for a second a young man tall dark and satanically handsome reaching up towards her.

The hatchway slides shut the invidious turns in the air and then blasts away and dematerialises and they are gone.

The tower explodes and disappears in a galactic pillar of fire.

INVIDIOUS MASTER CONTROL ROOM.

In the Invidious' control room John is scrabbling inside a locker. He emerges with an old-fashioned storm lantern an ancient atlas and an enormous book.

    John, Intensely, 'There's one chance. Just one...'

Kate looks down at her tattered sacrificial robe

 .
 Kate, 'Just don't tell me anything till I've had a wash and change okay?'

When Kate comes back into the control room she finds John has removed a small panel from a console, he is removing a small but complex, invidious circuitry and transferring it with enormous care to the interior of the big old storm lantern.

Kate watches him intrigued for a while and then she speaks...

Kate, 'Okay John. You can start by telling me how you whistled up the Invidious like that.'

John, 'The whistle was purely symbolic. It focused my mind while I sent out a powerful thought- impulse to the Invidious' telepathic circuits.'

Kate, 'So we could have got away from that ghastly place whenever we wanted to?

John, 'Well not really. We were observed and under guard for must of the time and I didn't dare risk-letting Kaiser get his hands on the Invidious.'

Kate, 'But we could have escaped long before we did? When we were first on the tower for instance?'

John, 'I didn't want to leave till I'd sorted things out. As it it all this is far from over.'

Kate, 'I thought we won?'

John, 'Not yet we haven't. Remember the Caretaker has control of Hitler's mind. When he figured out all was lost he made himself into pure energy massive and chose to use Hitler in finishing the Reckoning Movement and the Dark Dimension's evil plan.

If the Caretaker is anything like his father he won't stop at anything at fulfilling that destiny. Even if it means destroying himself in that process...

However I sense that because Hitler's mind is labyrinth of strength of madness the Caretaker has become trapped within its insane grip.

He has boosted Hitler's powers but he can't control him properly.

Hitler's mind is now controlling the Caretaker's soul the hunter has become the captive so to speak. It's using all of the Caretakers knowledge to help the Nazi's win the war.

The Caretaker forgot that mega maniacs like Hitler have a colossal strength of will.'

Kate, 'So Hitler gets to be a perfectly genuine superman? Using the mind of a trans- dimensional being from the Dark Dimension, that was trying to use him in the first place.'

John nods gloomily.

'It's a total disaster… Thanks to the mind of a trans- dimensional being, he's strong he's magnetic, he's confident he won't make any more crazy mistakes. He could stay on top forever.'

Kate, 'Looks like he's set up a winning combo John. So what are you going to do?'

John, 'There's just one chance left. If I can intervene just once more at precisely the right place and the right time…'

Kate, 'When and where?'

John consults his book.

Kate looks over his shoulder at the title of the book.

'The Day by Day Almanac of World War II'

John, 'We're going to a place codenamed 'Felsennest'. On a particular night in May 1940…'

Kate counts on her fingers.

Kate, 'That's what about nine months after we left? Can you time things that close?'

John gravely, 'I must, I must.'

John finishes his work on the storm lantern and snaps it shut. Kate looks curiously at the lantern.

Kate, 'and where does that thing come in to all this?'

John mysteriously, 'I shall use it to light up the dark recesses of Hitler's mind- and reveal the Caretaker in his real form. I will try to cloud Hitler's mind into thinking that I am a close friend and then when I am ready I will humiliate the Caretaker into showing itself. Because I think only rage will release it.'

. *'FELSENNEST'. HITLER'S COMMAND BUNKER. NIGHT.*

'Felsennest' the eyrie on the cliffs this is Adolf Hitler's command post.

It is late at night and Hitler dismisses his staff. He stands alone in his uniform tonic his 'soldiers coat' gazing out over the mountains and forests.

He isn't in the least surprised when John and Kate appear out of the night toiling up the mountainside. It is almost as if he is expecting them.

He opens the door and calls out to the suspicious sentry to let them in and to allow them to leave after their meeting with him, no matter what happens.

Once they are inside Hitler nods jovially at the glowing lantern in John's hand.

Hitler, 'You come to bring me light my friend?'

John sombrely, 'I hope so. How goes the war?'

Hitler, 'Very well, my friend very well indeed...'

He leads John and Kate to a wall map and picks up a pointer.

Hitler pointing at certain areas of the map, 'Poland is ours, of course. Holland and Belgium have been over- run and in France my armies have encircled the enemy and reached Abbeville, here. Boulogne and Calais have already fallen and General Guderian's Panzer Division is about to cut off the only remaining part some little place called...'

Hitler peers at the map.

'Dunkirk.'

John, 'A magnificent achievement... And the credit is yours- all yours... '

Hitler, 'Mine- and the power within me, my enlightened friend...'

John, 'You are too modest. The credit is yours. This so called power is nothing beside your towering genius.'

Hitler starts to look tense, uneasy, haunted...

Hitler, 'No, no my friend. The power within me must have its due.'

John, scornfully, 'What power? Some pathetic ghost wandering the universe looking for a free ride... I know all about him. Caretaker he calls himself. Well, the Caretaker is a accurate enough description for him, he has nothing better to do than to clean up other people's filth. He's nothing!'

John holds up the glowing lantern to illuminate Hitler's face. Suddenly Hitler goes rigid. His eyes glow brightly with strange light. Hitler opens his mouth to speak the voice of not the Caretaker but Stacey's comes from it...

Stacey, 'Nothing! Parker! You dare say I am nothing!'

John shocked, Stacey! But how?? Well you have been busy, and you are nothing and less than nothing... Still I suppose you've found your level, raised to the top like the cosmic scum you are.'

The eyes burn brighter. Hitler's whole body begins to glow.

John, 'But then what are you after all? A tame loser serving a petty human was lord helping him to rule this mud ball of a planet of ours.'

Adolf Hitler's body glows even brighter and it begins to change. It becomes a pillar of light and from that pillar emerges the metallic trans- dimensional form of Stacey a cross between a human form and a hideous nightmarish creation. It is a good seven feet tall, classically beautiful and totally terrifying.

Stacey, 'screaming in rage, 'A servant? I turned this pot- house politician this street- corner ranter into a man who could rule a country! Now if I choose I will give him a world, a galaxy! I will rule through him! Rule and destroy!'

John laughing loudly, 'Think about what you've become. You pathetic cosmic poltergeist, go and smash a few cups slam a few doors frighten people on the night. You're not a power you're just a petty nuisance. You bore me.'

Stacey hisses with rage.

John holds up his lantern to the tall silver form.

John, 'You're trapped in the mind of a mad man and you know it. Soon you will burn him out. As he grows older and madder and eventually dies you too will wither away…'

Pauses

'Of course, if you were to be housed in the mind of a powerful Enigma Federation member…that would be a great victory for the Dark Dimension. You wouldn't even need a Reckoning Movement anymore…'

Stacey, 'Do you offer me an alliance John Parker?'

John, 'I offer you a fair fight- here on your own ground, one and one, away from the Invidious. I can free you totally from this human's mind. Sever the link completely.'

Stacey, 'cutting in sharply, 'and then?'

John, 'My mind is yours- if you can take it.'

The Stacey's eyes glow with an eerie silver colour and John screams out in pain dropping his lantern. He holds his head in his hands as if trying to block out a terrible pain.

Kate picks up a chair and rushes over to the Stacey and smashes it over her body. Stacey lets out an inhuman scream and lashes out with its arm and knocks Kate aside like a flea.

Kate gets back to her feet and is about to attack the creature once more when she receives a telepathic message from John.

John, 'telepathically to Kate, 'don't get involved; trust me I know what I am doing. Whatever happens just stay out of its way?'

Stacey turns her attention back to John and touches his forehead. Energy runs down the length of the creatures arm making John convulse in pain. John holds his dignity and doesn't scream.

Stacey slaps John across the face seeming to enjoy watching John suffer at his hands.

Stacey screams at John, 'You did challenge me; you're nothing but a sorry excuse for a human being. Kneel before me and beg for a quick death before you willingly give me your power. Kneel and marvel at a true God.'

John doesn't kneel and gets up unsteadily to his feet; blood running from his nose and ears. Incredibly John laughs as if finding the whole thing highly amusing.

John, 'I will never kneel before you. You're nothing but like a child that can't have its own way. That's what you are a mere infant that hasn't grown up'.

Stacey hisses and lifts John up by the throat and stares deep into John's eyes with its hideous silver eyes. And then amazingly Stacey speaks gently to John.

Stacey, 'Give me what I desire and I shall spare your companion. Give it to me now, of your own free will.'

John defiantly shakes his head and spits at the creature.

Lighting bolts fire from the creatures' eyes and strike John. This time John does scream but manages to speak.

John screams in awful pain, 'Come on, surly you can do better than that. I thought you trans- dimensional beings were made of stronger stuff. '

Stacey has had enough and throws John to the floor and screams out in anger...

John notices the lantern lying by his side. He grabs it quickly and just as Stacey swoops down on John he thrusts the lantern full into the creatures' stomach.

The lantern glows with the brightness of a star, which can be seen within the transparent body of Stacey. The portrait of Hitler hung on the wall starts to melt and burn.

Stacey lashes about angrily, battering at some unseen pain – than suddenly there is a great burst of light and with a last terrible howl the thing that had once been Stacey explodes and then is gone.

Kate rushers over to John and hold him tight and then looks up angrily at him.

Kate, 'What the hell do you think you were doing? That thing almost killed you.'

John smiles a shaky smile at her and wipes away the blood from his face.

John, 'I had to weaken her enough so I could put the lantern with in her body...and the only way to do that was to blind her with rage. It was the only way if I had told you, you would never have gone along with the plan.'

Kate is about to say something when they both hear someone sobbing uncontrollably.

There on the floor crouching is Adolf Hitler. Now nothing but a broken man...

John walks over and lifts him into a seat.

Hitler, 'The power has left me. What must I do? Please tell me.'

John leans over him staring into the terrified eyes, speaking in a calm positive voice.

John, 'You must let the British Army go! Even though you are at war with the British you respect them you admire their Empire.
Let their army go home, postpone your invasion plan and eventually they will make peace with you. They will become your allies against Bolshevik hordes, your real enemy.'

Hitler, feverishly, 'Yes, yes, you are right.'

John hands him a field telephone.

John, 'You are the Fuehrer. Give the order.'

Hitler takes the phone and manages in a shaky version of his old commanding voice speech.

Hitler into phone, 'This is the Fuehrer. Send this message to General Guderian immediately. There is to be no further advance on Dunkirk. No further advance.'

John, 'That's the idea. Remember no advance on Dunkirk postpone the invasion of England... Come on Kate, we must go.'

Hitler looks up in alarm.

Hitler, 'You are leaving my friend? But what will become of me?'

John pauses for a moment in the doorway. He notices the handgun on the desk.

John, 'You will fulfil your destiny.'

John and Kate disappear into the night.

INVIVIOUS MASTER CONTROL ROOM.

John and Kate are once more back in the control room of the time ship and the Invidious is once again in flight. John looks gloomy and downcast.

Kate, 'Okay John talk.'

John, 'Talk, about what?'

Kate, 'the magic lantern for a start, what was it?'

John, 'A telepathic relay, I used it to extend the Invidious' force field. I tapped the power of the Invidious to help me free Stacey from Hitler's brain. When he attached me I boosted the power of the force field and it blew him away.'

Kate, 'So she's destroyed...'

John, 'Well, you might say she's gone all to pieces. I checked the time- path indicator. You see nothing. No reading...'

Kate, 'So where is she?'

John, 'Swirling round some void or another in an unfocused storm of pure anger. But her will to survive is enormous. She'll get herself together again in a millennium or two...'

Kate, 'So we haven't heard the last about that thing...'

John sighs, 'I doubt it. I couldn't even do that properly.'

Kate, 'Look, what's the matter with you John?'

John, 'It's all such a mess!'

Kate, 'What is?'

John, 'Bloody human history... We mangle ourselves quite enough if we're left alone. But this Reckoning Movement and the Dark Dimension interference Stacey's interference and then my cock- handed interference to sort everything out on top of all that.'

Kate, 'You did all you could John. That's all we can ever do.'

John, 'And look what came of it! I not only got one of the most terrible wars in human history back on the road. I freed that monster Stacey without completely destroying her for good. Trapped in Hitler's mind she might have withered away and died. Now she's still out there roaming the cosmos and dimensions and...'

John looks sadly at Kate, even more depressed.

And I doubt very much that Kaiser is truly gone as well. I have a feeling he exists in some form or another; ready to strike again.'

Kate stares at John uncomfortable with his words and then with a bright smile she goes over and hugs him, gives him a quick kiss on the cheek, trying to cheer him up.

Kate, 'Well at least you put history right...'

John, 'What's right about it? History's been mucked about so much who knows what's true and what's false. And who cares anyway?'

Kate, 'Come off it John, we know what's supposed to happen.'

John, 'Six years of war... Everything from the Holocaust to Hiroshima, with Dresden along the way! And I made sure it all happened on schedule!'

Kate, 'Where does Dresden come into it?'

John, 'Oh it was a pretty little historical beauty spot hammered into rubble for no good reason at all.'

Kate, frowns, 'Hang on, Dresden is in Germany, the Nazis wouldn't do that.'

John sadly, 'They didn't. Our lot did.'

Kate, sombrely, 'our side did Hiroshima as well and Nagasaki... But none of it's your fault John. All you did was put things back the way they were.

So the Nazis lost in 'forty five' and Adolf's 'Thousand Year Reich' fizzled out after twelve…Opening the way for a future, which produced wonderful things like the Enigma Federation and me.'

John, 'Ah but did it. The fabric of time was badly torn Kate. You can't stitch it up like repairing an old shirt. Suppose I made things even worse.'

Kate, 'Well let's go look and see.'

John, 'Where?'

Kate, '1951, the Festival of Britain…'

John, '1951? Are you sure? If history's been even mare radically altered it might not have produced you at all- you could disappear the minute we teleport down from the Invidious.'

Kate kisses John again on the cheek and pats his head.

Kate brightly, 'I'll risk it. Anything's better than travelling through time and space with a depressed old man. Let's get to that festival. And stop being so negative!'

John looks at her and manages a smile.

1951 THE FESTIVAL OF BRITAIN

SOUTH BANK. 1951. DAY.

The teleport gate appears on the south bank and John and Kate emerge. It is pouring with rain. John looks at Kate. Everything is it should be.

John, 'Well, you're still here.'

Kate, 'Told you, you can't get rid of me that easy. Well, you did it John. You put a stitch in time.'

John, 'Yes but I didn't do it alone, we both did it.'

Kate, 'This time we definitely did well!'

John puts up his umbrella.

John, 'Want to visit the Pavilion of the future?'

Kate, 'Well, I'm hungry. How do you English gentleman say? What about a cuppa and a bun?'

John laughs and kisses Kate on the forehead gently before answering.

John, 'Well as long as I don't have to hear you Americans asking me where you lot can get coffee and doughnuts.'

They both laugh as they make their way to a coffee stall where a cheerful little man is polishing teaspoons. A notice over his head reads:

THE COFFEE SHOP- H. GOLDSTEIN, PROP

Man, 'What can I get for you two nice people?'

John, 'Two teas and two buns, please...'

The little man serves their tea and buns. They ate and drink with great enjoyment.

John, 'Very good cup of tea this...'

Kate, 'Terrific bun...'

Man, 'Well they give us extra rations for the old Festival. Nice to be able to give people something decent for a change. You gotta admit it, things are getting better- slowly. Look its even stopped raining...'

John smiles and folds away his umbrella. A couple of yobs slouch over to the stall jostling Kate and John aside.

Yob 1, 'How about a free cuppa?'

Yob 2, 'and a pound out of the till... Come on all you lot are rolling in it.'

Kate clenches her fist and draws a deep breath. John touches her arm and speaks to her gently.

'Let him handle it Kate.'

Man, 'You Oppit! Before I come round there and clip your ear.'

Yob 1, 'You and who else?'

Kate taps him on the shoulder.

Kate points at John, 'Him and me for a start...'

John sighs and takes a firm grip on his umbrella. Then a policeman appears a large old- fashioned- type policeman from the 1950's.

Policeman, 'Is there any trouble here?'

The man laughs, 'Them? Trouble? I survived old' Itler's blitz, I should worry about the likes of them.'

The policeman stares at the youths and the two youths stare back absolutely terrified.

Policeman snaps, 'Oppit!'

The two yobs hop it.

The policeman watches as the youths run away and then turns to the stall keeper and breaks into a large smile, it's clear that he knows the stall keeper.

Policeman, 'All right. Harry?'

Man, 'Fine ta. Want a cuppa Joe?'

Police, 'Later maybe.'

The policeman touches his helmet and moves on. Dusk is falling and colour lights gleam in the distance.

John turns to the stall keeper.

John, 'What's that music?'

The little man stares at them in amazement.

Man, 'Where you been?'

Kate, 'You'd be surprised.'

Man, 'Got a funfair haven't they? Over in Battersea Park... All there years of post war austerity now it's all Festivals and funfairs... Funny old world... Innit?'

John, 'I like funfairs.'

He looks at Kate.

'Do you like funfairs?'

Kate, 'Yeah why not? Come on John.'

They say goodbye to the coffee stall man and stroll away.

Kate, 'He's right you know…'

John, 'Who is?'

Kate, 'the coffee stall man; It is a funny old world.'

John, 'I know. But it could have been a lot worse…'

Kate, 'Well it has been hasn't it? But we sorted that out, like I said we did well.'

She grins at John and he grins back. He looks thoughtful for a moment.

John, 'After the funfair there's a little something I have to do…'

Kate, 'And what would that be?'

John smiles, 'Get back to a dinner date in England, Southampton in the year 2015.

THE BLACK CAT BAR/RESTAURANT. NIGHT.

We are back where we started the script in 'The Black Cat' bar. Kim is looking at John worried.

John speaking as if in a great deal of pain, 'God what's happening to me? Please Kim I think I need a Doctor.'

John disappears for a moment his image flickers like a bad television picture. Then he is back, whole again. He looks at Kim, with a cheerful expression. Kim just stares at him. After a moment she speaks…

Kim, 'What's going on? I swear for a moment you disappeared right before my eyes.'

John, 'Well, I'm back now. You must have been seeing things.'

Kim, 'Ah… you said you needed a doctor?'

John, 'Did I? Oh just an upset belly, it's passed now. Listen would you like some more wine?'

Kim, 'No, I think I've had enough.'

Kim and John both hear a voice.

'Sorry I'm late.'

John and Kim look up. There standing by their table is Kate Anderson looking lovely in a black dress. John smiles and then notices Kim staring at him and Kate as if to say 'Who is this?'

John, 'Oh forgive me Kim. This is my wonderful girlfriend Kate Anderson, I'm sure you'll like her. She's a great help. Please Kate take a seat.'

Kate takes a seat at the table and looks around.

Kate, 'Bit creepy here isn't it?'

Kim, 'Funny John was saying the same thing. Well I must say John is a dark horse, he never told me about you. Aren't you lovely? He's landed on his feet with you I must say.'

Kate, 'You're very kind.'

Kim, 'Look I'll just go to the bar and get us some drinks, what would you like Kate?'

Kate, 'Whiskey with coke please… it's been a hard day not to mention a hard decade or two lately… '

Kim stares at them unsure what to make of what Kate just said, so she smiles at John and asks…

Kim, 'Soft drink for you John?'

John, 'Like always Kim…'

Kim goes after leaving the couple alone. John takes out a cigarette lights it and looks at Kate through the smoke. It is clear she has something on her mind…

John, 'Penny for your thoughts?'

Kate, 'I was just thinking there's more to you than meets the eye. I have a feeling you're much more than just an Enigma Federation member.'

John, 'What makes you say that?'

Kate, 'I don't know, but it's just a feeling I have. And I trust my feelings. I know for a fact you're a good kind man. But like I said I think there's more to you than meets the eye.'

John, 'There's an old saying that goes 'Ask no questions and I'll tell you no lies'

Kate smiles fondly at John.

Kate, 'One day you'll have to tell me some of your secrets. I can wait I have all the time in the world.'

John smiles and winks at her.

John, 'Yes we have all the time in the world...'

John leans over and kisses Kate romantically.

DARK DIMENSION

We are on some strange surreal planet within the Dark Dimension. A massive fleet of huge futuristic war ships hang suspended in a violent red sky. From below the entities that had one been Kaiser and the Caretaker watch proudly a large triangle of light appears before them.

And a metallic and horrifying classically beautiful but nightmarish version of the being that had once been Stacey Cannon emerges from the triangle of light.

The Kaiser and Caretaker entities kneel before the nightmarish Stacy Cannon, she speaks to them in an icily beautiful voice that is cold and silvery and eerily metallic.

Stacey, 'Soon my children we will have our revenge against the weak souls of mankind and other species that dare stand in our way. We will destroy John Parker by taking away everything that is close to him...'

The entity that was once Stacey Cannon stares up at the fleet of ships that hang suspended in the sky...

Stacey, 'Soon the Dimension Wars will begin and we shall start off by destroying the almighty Enigma Federation. I have been mocked humiliated for the last time by the Enigma Federation once they are back in my power I will make them beg for death and deny them. In time I will annihilate them.'

She screams in a hideous roar.

'Send out the Dimension Time War Ships…'

The massive frightening fleet of war ships blast off and disappear.

The End??